Risking
– the –
Forbidden Game

Trailblazer Books

Gladys Aylward • *Flight of the Fugitives*
Mary McLeod Bethune • *Defeat of the Ghost Riders*
William & Catherine Booth • *Kidnapped by River Rats*
Charles Loring Brace • *Roundup of the Street Rovers*
Governor William Bradford • *The Mayflower Secret*
John Bunyan • *Traitor in the Tower*
Amy Carmichael • *The Hidden Jewel**
Peter Cartwright • *Abandoned on the Wild Frontier*
George Washington Carver • *The Forty-Acre Swindle*
Maude Cary • *Risking the Forbidden Game*
Elizabeth Fry • *The Thieves of Tyburn Square*
Jonathan & Rosalind Goforth • *Mask of the Wolf Boy*
Barbrooke Grubb • *Ambushed in Jaguar Swamp*
Sheldon Jackson • *The Gold Miners' Rescue*
Adoniram & Ann Judson • *Imprisoned in the Golden City*
Festo Kivengere • *Assassins in the Cathedral*
David Livingstone • *Escape From the Slave Traders**
Martin Luther • *Spy for the Night Riders**
Dwight L. Moody • *Danger on the Flying Trapeze*
Lottie Moon • *Drawn by a China Moon*
Samuel Morris • *Quest for the Lost Prince*
George Müller • *The Bandit of Ashley Downs*
John Newton • *The Runaway's Revenge*
Florence Nightingale • *The Drummer Boy's Battle*
John G. Paton • *Sinking the Dayspring*
William Penn • *Hostage on the Nighthawk*
Joy Ridderhof • *Race for the Record*
Nate Saint • *The Fate of the Yellow Woodbee*
Rómulo Sauñe • *Blinded by the Shining Path*
William Seymour • *Journey to the End of the Earth*
Menno Simons • *The Betrayer's Fortune*
Mary Slessor • *Trial by Poison*
Hudson Taylor • *Shanghaied to China**
Harriet Tubman • *Listen for the Whippoorwill*
William Tyndale • *The Queen's Smuggler*
John Wesley • *The Chimney Sweep's Ransom*
Marcus & Narcissa Whitman • *Attack in the Rye Grass*
David Zeisberger • *The Warrior's Challenge*

Hero Tales: A Family Treasury of True Stories
From the Lives of Christian Heroes (Volumes I, II, III, & IV)

*Curriculum guide available.
Written by Julia Pferdehirt with Dave & Neta Jackson.

Risking
– the –
Forbidden Game

Dave & Neta Jackson

Illustrated by Anne Gavitt

BETHANY HOUSE PUBLISHERS
MINNEAPOLIS, MINNESOTA 55438

Risking the Forbidden Game
Copyright © 2002
Dave and Neta Jackson

Illustrations © 2002
Bethany House Publishers

Story illustrations by Anne Gavitt.
Cover design and illustration by Catherine Reishus McLaughlin.

Scripture quotations are from the King James Version of the Bible.

Published by Bethany House Publishers
A Ministry of Bethany Fellowship International
11400 Hampshire Avenue South
Bloomington, Minnesota 55438
www.bethanyhouse.com

Printed in the United States of America by
Bethany Press International, Bloomington, Minnesota 55438

Library of Congress Cataloging-in-Publication Data

Jackson, Dave.
    Risking the forbidden game : Maude Cary / by Dave & Neta Jackson ; illustrations by Anne Gavitt.
        p.   cm. — (Trailblazer books)
    Summary: A Muslim boy, in Morocco, risks his parent's wrath when he accepts pictures of Jesus from a Christian missionary named Maude Cary.
    ISBN 0-7642-2234-1
    1. Cary, Maude, d. 1967—Juvenile fiction. [1. Cary, Maude, d. 1967—Fiction. 2. Muslims—Fiction. 3. Missionaries—Fiction. 4. Morocco—History—20th century—Fiction. 5. Christian life—Fiction.] I. Jackson, Neta. II. Gavitt, Anne, ill. III. Title. IV. Series: Jackson, Dave. Trailblazer books.
PZ7.J132418   Ri   2002
[Fic]—dc21
                                                    2002009987

This story about Maude Cary, missionary to Morocco, takes place in the spring of 1925, when Abd el-Krim, "the Desert Prince," fomented rebellion against the French. The German deserter, Sgt. Joseph Klem, who aided the rebellion, as well as all dates and battles are documented in fact.

Into this historical time frame we weave a fictional story about a "forbidden game" to highlight the tensions between the Muslim population and their French "protectors," and between three faiths: Islam, Judaism, and Christianity.

Jamal Isaam and his friend Hameem are fictional characters loosely based on two real Muslim boys in Sefrou—Mehdi Ksara and Mohammed Bouabid—who attended Miss Cary's school and eventually became Christians and co-workers with her. The soldier, David Hoffman, is also based on a true character named Leon Feldman, a Polish Jew who deserted the French Foreign Legion in Morocco, was converted, and also became one of Maude Cary's faithful co-workers. (See "More About Maude Cary" for more information about these historical characters.) However, the relationship between the boys, the soldier, and their game is entirely fictional.

Find us on the Web at . . .

TrailblazerBooks.com

- Meet the authors.

- Read the first chapter of each book—
  with the pictures.

- Track the Trailblazers around the world
  on a map.

- Use the historical timeline to find out
  what other important events were happening in the world at the time of each
  Trailblazer story.

- Discover how the authors research their
  books, and link to some of the same
  sources they used, where
  you can learn more
  about these heroes.

- Write to the authors.

- Explore frequently asked
  questions about writing
  and Trailblazer books.

Just point your browser to *www.trailblazerbooks.com*

CONTENTS

DAVE AND NETA JACKSON are a full-time husband/wife writing team who have authored and coauthored many books on marriage and family, the church, relationships, and other subjects. Their books for children include the TRAILBLAZER series and *Hero Tales,* volumes I, II, III, and IV. The Jacksons make their home in Evanston, Illinois.

Chapter 1

The Dare

An overloaded donkey heaved an annoyed *eee-aww! eee-aww!* in the narrow cobblestone street below the second-floor window, waking Jamal from his dreams. But as soon as the boy popped his eyes open, he heard the familiar call of the *muezzin* from the tall minaret of the mosque in the square: "Allah is great! There is no God but Allah!"

The morning call to prayer already? Jamal sat bolt upright on the soft rugs and cushions that served as his bed and squinted at his uncle Samir's bed in the semi-dark room. Empty.

Jamal groaned and felt around for his trousers and cloth shoes. Why hadn't he heard Uncle Samir leave for prayer? He had wanted to get up in time to grab a handful of dates and drink some water before the gray fingers of dawn revealed "the difference between a black thread and a white thread"—the traditional way in the Muslim world to tell when another day of fasting had begun during the month of Ramadan. Now there would be nothing to eat or drink until nightfall.

Winding his cloth sash around his already rumbling belly, Jamal hurried out on the balcony that ringed the second floor of rooms above the open courtyard of the Isaam home. The household was quiet. His father, grandfather, and uncle were probably already at the mosque where his father led prayers five times a day. His younger sisters were probably still asleep—still "babies" needing to be cared for by their mother.

Jamal hurried down the steps to the lower courtyard, padded across the cool tiles and through the dark hall to the front door. It wasn't easy not to eat or drink all day long during Ramadan, but he was twelve now, no longer a child for whom exceptions could be made. Well, he'd just have to tough it out till his family broke the fast at nightfall . . . but all the more reason to play The Game today. It helped distract his mind from his empty stomach.

A smile tugged at the corners of Jamal's mouth as he slipped out the door and ran down the narrow street to the mosque. No one else knew about The Game except his friend Hameem. It all started a couple weeks back when the two boys, playing along the river that flowed down the mountain and watered the town of Sefrou, had found a military canteen stuck in the mud of the riverbank. . . .

Jamal snatched up the canteen, looking around to see if anyone had seen him. One of the French soldiers occupying the town must have dropped it.

Hameem's eyes grew wide as Jamal dipped the canteen in the cold, rushing river, then raised it to his lips to drink. "What are you doing, foolish boy! That belongs to the infidels!"

Jamal, a wiry contrast to the stocky Hameem, shrugged. "It's mine now."

"But if they catch you with it, they will think you are a thief!"

Jamal considered. He knew the rules. French property was French property and should be returned to the commanding officer. But why should he help the French? The French didn't belong in Sefrou—or anywhere in Morocco, for that matter. That's what Uncle Samir said. Jamal's uncle agreed with the rebel tribes out in the desert who refused to accept the Treaty of Fez the sultan had signed in 1912, which made Morocco a French Protectorate. For the most part, French, Arab, African, and Jew mingled side by side in the walled cities and towns along Morocco's fertile coastal plains. But the wild Berber tribes—who barely accepted the sultan's authority, much less a foreign power—kept the spirit of rebellion alive. One day Morocco would be independent once more.

Jamal decided. "It's my trophy—the spoil of war!" He held the canteen high.

Hameem sneered. "Do you think your uncle will let you bring that into your house? Your mother will make you wash your hands and say ten prayers of penitence."

That was true, too. The sultans of Morocco might be pro-European, with their phonographs and railroads and electric lights. And ordinary Muslims tolerated and cooperated with their French "protectors." But many devout Muslims would not allow *anything* belonging to the infidels in that most sacred place, their homes.

Jamal pulled Hameem down into the scrubby

bushes, where they could not be seen by the women washing clothes in the river. His dark eyes shone with an idea. "Hameem! We can pretend we are rebels, fighting alongside the Desert Prince." Uncle Samir had often held the boys spellbound with stories about the exploits of Abd el-Krim, the notorious rebel leader among the Berber tribes. "It will be a contest—just between you and me—to see who can collect the most things belonging to the enemy." Jamal looked at Hameem's dubious face. "I dare you! Here—you can have the canteen to start your collection. Now you're ahead. But I'm going to win!"

And so The Game had started. Already Jamal had a plastic comb, a leather strap from an officer's horse, two empty bullet casings, and a metal fork in his treasure box, hidden under the bed pillows in his room. The boys had agreed on a point system: one point for something found; five points for something taken from the buildings the French occupied at the far end of Sefrou; and ten points for something lifted right off a French soldier.

As Jamal slipped into the big open room of the mosque where his father was leading the morning prayers, his mind was already plotting how he could add to his collection after school. But catching the disapproving look in his grandfather's eye, Jamal quickly washed his hands for the ritual cleansing, then slipped to his knees facing the *mihrab,* the niche in the far wall that pointed the way to Mecca, the Holy City.

✧ ✧ ✧ ✧

Jamal was afraid he'd be scolded for being late to morning prayer, but his father, grandfather, and uncle were already arguing as the Isaam men headed back to their household—as if morning prayer had interrupted a conversation already in progress.

"Samir, you see a rebellion under every rock in the desert." Jamal's father, the *imam,* or leader of prayers in the mosque, waved a hand as though brushing off Samir's words.

"And *you* wouldn't recognize a rebellion if it sat in your courtyard and ate from your dish, Mirsab!" scowled his brother. Uncle Samir was the younger of the two Isaam brothers, but his muscles were big and hard and he walked with a swagger. Jamal had always thought of him as a giant of a man.

"My son, *why* do you think el-Krim is planning a major attack?" said Grandfather Hatim mildly. "We hear rumors all the time. Nothing comes of them."

"Because of *that.*" Uncle Samir pointed to a piece of paper tacked to the wall of the corner house on the square. Jamal ran over to look. The face of a French soldier stared from the poster. The writing beneath was in both French and Arabic: "WANTED—for desertion and treason. Sgt. Joseph Klem, 2nd Régiment Étranger d'Infanterie. REWARD." The poster was dated April 1925—the European calendar.

"So?" shrugged Jamal's father. "French soldiers desert all the time."

Uncle Samir lowered his voice. "But *this* one has

joined forces with Abd el-Krim. He knows weapons—now el-Krim's forces can be trained to use the machine guns and artillery they took from the Spanish."

Jamal's father snorted. "Ha. Not very likely."

Grandfather Hatim's voice was still mild, soothing. "But the last we heard of el-Krim, he was far to the north in the Rif Mountains. And besides, surely no one would mount a major offensive during Ramadan." Jamal's grandfather was a respected judge in Sefrou, and he approached all of life with a calm reason. He alone of the Isaam family had made a pilgrimage, a *hajj*, to Mecca, the holy city in Saudi Arabia.

"An excellent time in my opinion!" growled Uncle Samir. "We are not distracted by our bellies or women. Don't say I didn't—"

"Come, come, no more talk of war and rebellion," said Grandfather. The men had arrived at the blue door in the whitewashed wall that led into the spacious home within. "We do not want to upset Faheema and the little ones. Mirsab, I will not be back until time for *iftar* this evening—the French magistrate and I have a full load of cases today. . . . Jamal? Can you be ready in half an hour? I will walk you back to school."

Jamal tried to concentrate as the thin-faced teacher paced back and forth in front of the school-room, part of the mosque in the square, chanting

15

that day's verses from the Koran. " 'This is why when Allah prescribed fasting, he says: "O you who believe! Fasting is prescribed to you as it was prescribed to those before you, that you may learn self- restraint." ' "

" 'This is why when Allah prescribed fasting . . .' " the roomful of boys repeated.

"Where is it found?" demanded the teacher.

"Al-Qur'an, 2:184," said the boys dutifully.

The teacher continued to pace, his brown striped *jellaba,* the long hooded robe worn by most Muslim men, moving back and forth across Jamal's vision like a long loaf of bread. Jamal shook his head. He mustn't think about food.

"Get out your number boards."

The room erupted in a shuffle as boys pulled clay-covered boards from beneath their benches. Jamal glanced at Hameem. His friend was already at work with a thin wooden stylus, pressing the number problems given by the teacher into the soft clay. Jamal sighed. Why was the morning going so slowly?

The last lesson of the day was French. Jamal groaned silently. Arabic was hard enough. Why did they have to learn to read and write French? The letters and words didn't even use the same alphabet!

Finally the call of the *muezzin* floated through the windows: "Allah is great! There is no God but Allah!" Time for midday prayers. School was over.

Benches were hurriedly moved aside, prayer rugs laid side by side, and the teacher, also an *imam,* led the boys in the second set of the daily prayers.

Then, like horses released from a starting gate, the boys poured from the schoolroom into the square and galloped eagerly toward freedom. Jamal grabbed Hameem and pulled him down the congested street. "Want to back out?"

Hameem shook his head, and the boys took off running. Since there was no noon meal—the main meal for most Muslim families—during Ramadan, the boys had agreed to scout out the French quarters today to see what they could find to add to their "booty" collections. So far, pointwise, they were neck and neck. It was time to take The Game to a new level.

As usual, the streets were full of merchants selling their wares in the daily *suqs,* or markets, along with jugglers, musicians, and storytellers. Some merchants were shutting down until after mid-afternoon prayers, when business would pick up again. Each street market boasted different goods for sale—baskets in one *suq*; grains, herbs, and spices in another; bolts of cloth and embroidered clothing in another. Jamal deliberately avoided the market selling fresh food. The smell of *couscous* and *tajins*—a savory stew of mutton and vegetables—simmering in their pots could be his undoing. *I can wait till nightfall,* Jamal muttered to himself.

"Hey!" said Hameem. "Look."

The boys stopped to check out the small crowd that had gathered around two brown-haired men standing on wooden crates right in the middle of the basket *suq*. One was wearing a traditional *jellaba,* but the other had on long trousers and a long-sleeved shirt. Not far away, a middle-aged woman sat in the doorway of an abandoned barbershop, passing out picture postcards to a group of boys. She wore a blue caftan like most Moroccan women, but her hair was brown, her face uncovered and pale. Probably American.

Curious, the boys stood on tiptoe at the back of the crowd, trying to hear what was going on. The brown-haired men spoke in careful Arabic, as though the language was unfamiliar.

"Ever since the time of our father Abraham, the prophets in the Old Testament spoke of a Messiah, who would save the people from their sins. Jesus Christ, the Son of God, came to—"

Jamal poked Hameem and snickered behind his hand. He knew most European or American foreigners were Christian—at least, they weren't Muslim. But he'd never heard any of them actually talk about the Christian God.

"Son of God?" challenged a voice in the crowd. "There is only one God, and Allah is his name!"

"You are right, my friend—there is only one God. But God has revealed himself in three persons—the Father, Jesus Christ the Son who lived among us, and the—"

"What nonsense is *that*?" another man called out. "One God, or three gods? The Koran says that Allah is God and Mohammed is his prophet."

"The Jews still wait for the Messiah!"

Jamal couldn't see the last speaker, but he was

probably from the *mellah,* the Jewish section of Sefrou.

The noises of merchants shutting down their shops and the clatter of donkey carts on the cobblestones made it hard to hear what the men were saying. Behind him, Jamal heard the woman's voice rise and fall, as though telling a story—a common pastime in the marketplace. Losing interest in the men's argument, Jamal pulled Hameem over to hear what the woman was saying. She was holding a large picture of a bearded man dressed in a *jellaba* and carrying a lamb on his shoulders. One of the boys dropped his postcard, and the wind skittered it against Jamal's foot. He bent down and picked it up. It was a copy of the same picture.

"The Good Shepherd looks for His lost sheep until He finds it, just like the shepherds here in Morocco count their sheep and goats each day and know if one is missing," the woman was saying in Arabic. But just then her pleasant voice was drowned out by the now-familiar *tramp, tramp, tramp* of soldiers marching through the marketplace.

Immediately the crowd parted and made room for the French Legionnaires. The soldiers wore blue caps with black bills and a square of fluttering cloth from the back that covered their necks from the hot Moroccan sun. Marching two abreast, they carried rifles over the left shoulder of their short, blue jackets, and their white pants were tucked into the top of black, shiny boots. A sergeant marked time at the head of the column: *"Un, deux, trois, quatre . . . Un, deux, trois, quatre . . ."*

The men in the market stared, then began to murmur among themselves. Jamal knew what they were thinking. Were these new recruits being assigned to Sefrou? Why? Did that mean the rumors of a rebellion in the Rif Mountains were true? Was Abd el-Krim on the move?

Jamal absently stuck the postcard in the folds of his sash just as something bright caught his eye—a loose button on the jacket of one of the French soldiers marching past him. It bounced on its threads, shining gold in the midday sun. *One point for something found, five points for something taken from the soldiers' quarters, ten points for taking something right off the soldier's person.*

With a sudden movement, Jamal darted close to the soldier, grabbed the button, and pulled. The button came off in his hand.

"Run!" he yelled to Hameem.

Chapter 2

The Forbidden Pictures

Ten points! Ten points!" Jamal danced gleefully around Hameem, waving the prized button in his friend's flushed face.

Still panting after their mad dash, the stocky Hameem rested his hands on his knees. Someone had yelled in French, "*Arrêtez!* Stop!" as the boys took flight. But they had zig-zagged through the marketplace, cut through a long alley, and lost themselves in another street full of copper pots, gleaming jewelry, and decorative metalwork. The coppersmiths' *suq*. At last they'd stopped to catch their breath.

Hameem did not join in Jamal's celebration dance. "If you're going to get us in trouble, you could at least give me some warning," he sulked.

Jamal just grinned. "Ho, ho! Pulled this button right off his jacket. How are you going to top *that*, eh? . . . Hey! Where are you going?"

"Home. I've got to help *Om* fill the water jugs."

"Huh. You didn't say anything about helping your mother when we were going to scout out the French quarters."

Hameem just shrugged. "See you tomorrow."

Jamal watched his friend make his way through the *suq*, which was emptying out for the midday rest period. Stubborn donkey. He'd won his ten points fair and square.

The midday sun was hot, even for early spring. Jamal was suddenly aware of how thirsty he was. A drink of water from the jugs his mother filled each day rose up in his mind like an oasis in the desert . . . and just as rapidly disappeared. No. No water to drink. Not until nightfall. The month of Ramadan was only ten days old, and he would have to learn to wait.

Jamal sauntered lazily toward his own house. From the outside, the Isaam home—like all the other homes along the narrow cobblestone street—looked blank and bare, a long whitewashed wall extending from one end of the street to where it opened into the square, punctuated with painted doorways. Behind the plain blue door, however, the Isaam home had welcoming cool, decorative tiles along the passageways, soft rugs, low tables, and bright cushions in the main family room, pots of green plants decorating the sunny courtyard, and waterfalls of ivy spilling from the balcony railings looking down into the courtyard from the second floor of rooms.

Jamal's little sisters pounced on him as he entered the courtyard, giggling. He picked up three-year-old Jasmine—"little flower"—and tickled her till she screamed with delight. Seven-year-old Jawhara's cheeks were stuffed with dates, and she sucked the sticky fruit off her fingers.

Lucky little goats. They didn't have to fast during Ramadan until they'd reached their womanhood.

Jamal untangled himself from Jasmine's clutches and ran up the courtyard stairs to the sleeping room he shared with Uncle Samir. Good. The room was empty. Jamal dug beneath a pile of cushions and blankets stacked in one corner and dragged out a small wicker chest with a rounded top. He opened the lid and dropped the button inside, where it nested with the black comb, empty shell casings, leather strap, and metal fork he'd found scouting the stables and barracks of the French Foreign Legion. He grinned. That button was worth more points than all the rest of them put together.

As Jamal closed the chest, a white postcard fluttered to the floor. What? He picked it up and turned it over. It was the picture of the shepherd carrying a lamb across his shoulders. He'd forgotten he'd tucked it into his cloth sash.

Jamal squinted his eyes and studied the picture in the dim light. Who was the bearded man? Must be a Berber tribesman—the man was out in the wild, with craggy rocks and scrubby bushes on all sides.

He was wearing a long robe, a cloth headdress, and sandals on his feet.

Why was the American woman telling stories about a Berber shepherd? Who was she, anyway? How long had she been living in Sefrou? Was she the wife of one of the men who'd been preaching Christianity?

Jamal shrugged to himself and dropped the picture into the chest along with the button. Maybe it would count for one point, since he'd found it in the street and it belonged to an infidel.

Jamal dipped his flatbread into the big bowl of steaming *tajins* in the middle of the low table and scooped up a mouthful. *Ahhh*. His mother's mutton stew, fragrant with onions and dried raisins, tasted especially good after going hungry all day. He quickly dipped again, fearing Uncle Samir and the friend he'd brought home with him after evening prayers might finish it off before he'd stilled the gnawing in his belly.

Faheema Isaam gave her oldest child a gentle scold with her eyes, then she smiled. Jamal relaxed. He knew what that smile meant: *Do not worry, there is plenty.* Of course. His mother always made a lot of food each evening during Ramadan, as it was common to invite guests to share *iftar,* the breaking of the fast.

Finally Grandfather Hatim leaned back against the cushions, content. It was the signal to clear the table of the big bowl they all ate from and bring out the tea. Jamal watched as his mother poured the steaming mint tea from the tall silver teapot and handed the small cups first to Samir's guest, then to the rest of the household. The tea was already plenty sweet, but Jamal snitched another sugar cone and dropped it into his cup.

After-dinner tea was the time for conversation. Uncle Samir's friend wiped the sugary tea from his shaggy beard. "The Christian missionaries were preaching in the marketplace again."

Jamal nearly choked on his tea. Hot liquid splashed on his shirt and up his nose. He forced a cough or two to cover up his alarm.

"Jamal! Are you all right?" Grandfather leaned toward him in concern.

"I—I'm fine, Grandfather." Jamal wiped his mouth with his sleeve and took another casual sip of tea. But his mind was racing. Had someone seen him rip that button off the uniform of the French soldier?

But the dark-eyed young man at Uncle Samir's side did not even glance at Jamal. "All their talk about a three-headed God—what blasphemy."

"One God in three persons, Mateen," Grandfather Hatim said gently to their guest. "If you are going to criticize another religion, at least get it right."

Uncle Samir snorted. "With all due respect, Father, you are too patient with these infidels! The Christians say they worship the one true God, but they are nothing but barbaric idol worshippers. Haven't you seen the statue in the chapel at French headquarters? Their Jesus is nailed to a cross, dying

25

like a common criminal. They even wear the gory image around their necks!"

Jamal was all ears. So *that's* what hung on a chain around the necks of some of the Legionnaires. He shivered in fascinated horror, just like the time he'd seen the heads of some Berber tribesmen hanging from the gates of Fez after clashes with the sultan's troops.

But he wasn't prepared for Mateen's next verbal shot. "*I* have heard that the Christians kill Muslim children if they catch them alone."

"All right, Mateen, that's enough!" said Jamal's father, gruffly. "You are a guest in our home, but I will not have my children frightened by careless rumors." Mirsab Isaam pointed a finger at his brother. "Samir, you and your friends do Islam no favors by refusing to get along with the foreigners among us. If we wish the Jews and the Christians to treat Islam with respect, we must respect their beliefs, as well. Debate is healthy! But it must be based on truth, not rumors."

"Truth?" Samir snorted. "I don't need the infidels' 'truth,' Mirsab. This is Morocco, and the Koran tells us all the truth we need to know."

The next day during school, Jamal was still thinking about what Uncle Samir and Mateen had said about the Christians, when he noticed that Hameem kept looking at him from the next row of benches.

Was Hameem still mad at him for getting that ten-point button? But his friend had a silly grin on his round face, as though he had a secret to tell. Jamal shot him a look: *What is it?* But Hameem ducked his head just as Jamal heard the whistle of the teacher's cane and felt its stinging *whack* on his shoulder.

"Pay attention to your own work, Jamal Isaam!" the teacher barked, then continued pacing up and down among the rows of benches. Jamal's face turned red as he struggled to keep tears from springing from his eyes. The sting in his shoulder was nothing compared to the fear that the teacher might tell his father he had misbehaved in school. Mirsab Isaam expected strict obedience from his children, and Jamal's punishment would be severe if the teacher complained about him.

Finally the sweet notes of the *muezzin* called them to midday prayer. Once the stampede of boys had emptied the schoolroom, Hameem fell into step beside Jamal. "I am sorry the teacher caned you."

Angry words leapt to Jamal's tongue, but Hameem truly looked sorry. "All right," he relented. "We are even now." More than even, Jamal thought. Making Hameem run from the French man yesterday wasn't half as bad as getting caned by the teacher.

Relieved, the same grin sprang to Hameem's lips.

"Why are you looking at me like a camel about to spit?" demanded Jamal.

Hameem's grin widened. "Come on, I'll show you!"

Curious, Jamal followed Hameem as he led the

way through the heart of the *medina,* the "old city," then stopped triumphantly outside an ordinary house. But strangely, the door stood open, and Jamal could hear children singing.

"What is this? It sounds like a school." Jamal tried to peer inside the open door into the dim passageway.

Hameem pulled him aside. "It is! It's the American woman's school," he hissed in Jamal's ear. "And I'm going in to see what it's all about. Now *that* ought to be worth ten points!" Hameem crossed his arms and tilted his chin up defiantly.

So that was what this was about—Hameem was trying to top the button episode yesterday. "Don't be a fool!" Jamal grabbed Hameem's shirt and tried to pull him away, but Hameem's stocky build did not budge. Instead, Hameem jerked away, gave Jamal a cocky grin over his shoulder, and disappeared into the open door.

Jamal stared after his friend, open-mouthed. School? What kind of school? The Islamic school was the only kind of school he knew about. He had an urge to march in after Hameem—after all, *he* was usually the one who dared to bend the rules and take a few risks for the sake of The Game.

But he hadn't had time to think this through. The American woman was probably a Christian—which made her an infidel. He was sure his father would say it was one thing to listen to the Christians in the open market, but quite another to go into their homes and attend their schools!

What *was* Hameem doing? As the minutes crawled by, Jamal paced up and down the street, though avoiding the front of the American woman's house. He was half mad at himself for not going in, too—would Hameem think he was a coward?—and half worried for Hameem. What if . . . what if the rumor about what happened to Muslim children if Christians got hold of them was true!

The sun had moved a good hour and Jamal was hot, thirsty, and irritable before Hameem appeared again in the doorway, along with several other Muslim and Jewish boys. The same American woman who had been telling stories in the basket *suq* yesterday came to the door and waved. *"Ma'a el salama!* Good-bye!"

This time Hameem allowed himself to be pulled along as Jamal grabbed his arm and towed him out of sight of the house. "What happened! Tell me!"

"Ten points?"

Jamal rolled his eyes. "All *right*. Ten points."

Hameem strolled slowly down the street. "Well, school today was called Sunday school—it is the Christians' holy day, the first day of their week."

Jamal frowned, puzzled. Islam's holy day was Friday. And that was the only day they did *not* have to go to school. "What did you do?"

"Well, she talked about the Christian Bible—"

"You mean you memorized verses from the Bible?" Memorizing verses from the Koran took up a major part of Islamic school.

"No. She just told us a story—about Jesus. The one they call the Son of God." Hameem dug in his

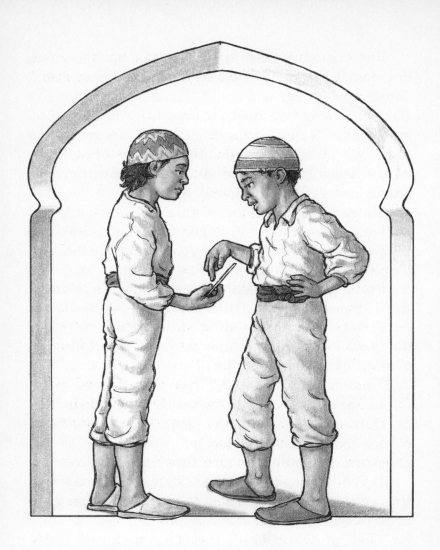

sash and pulled out a postcard. "I got a picture, too."

Jamal sucked in his breath. "Hameem! You better be careful! What would your father do if he found out you had gone inside the infidel's house and attended their Sunday school?"

Hameem shrugged, trying to look unconcerned, but Jamal caught the uneasy frown. "What else?" Jamal demanded.

"Well, Sunday school only meets on Sunday. But Miss Cary—that's her name—told us that she runs a school every afternoon for anyone who needs help with their regular school studies so they can pass their exams. She can speak three languages—English, French, and Arabic. And some Berber, too."

The boys walked in silence for a few moments. Then Hameem said, "Do you want to see the picture?" He thrust the postcard at Jamal.

Jamal studied the picture postcard. The bearded man—the same one who looked like a Berber shepherd—was holding a handful of mud and putting a mudpack on a man's eyes who was kneeling in front of him, his face upturned.

"That man was blind," Hameem offered helpfully. "Miss Cary told a story about how Jesus healed his eyes. She said if I come back she has lots more stories . . . and pictures, too."

Jamal wished he'd heard the story—but even as he studied the picture, a sly idea began to form. Hameem may have earned ten points for going to Miss Cary's Sunday school . . . but he, Jamal, could top *that* by collecting *all* the Jesus pictures! There had to be more. But he had to be careful—he would be in big trouble if his parents found them, not to mention Uncle Samir. But what was The Game if it didn't involve a dare? He already had one picture, and here was another. . . .

"Hameem." Jamal laid a hand on his friend's shoulder. "You really played The Game today—you earned that ten points! But don't take the Jesus picture home, or your parents may discover what you did. I don't want you to get in trouble because of The Game. Here—I'll get rid of this for you."

Before Hameem had time to think about it, Jamal tucked the picture into his sash and hollered, "Come on! I'll race you home!"

Chapter 3

The Infidel's School

There was only one way to get the American woman's Jesus pictures—Jamal would have to go to her afternoon school.

The more he thought about it, the more he was confident he could pull it off. After all, nothing had happened to Hameem, and he had gone to *Sunday* school. Jamal could go between prayer at noon and mid-afternoon prayer, when the boys were usually free to roam the marketplace or play outside the city gates anyway. No one would miss him as long as he showed up for the daily prayers.

Besides, hadn't Hameem said that Miss Cary offered to help with their regular studies—

Arabic, French, and numbers—so they could pass their exams? Both Grandfather Hatim and his father were expecting him to go to school in Fez after he passed Islamic school examinations. But Jamal often worried: what if he didn't pass?

The next day, the twelfth day of Ramadan, Jamal caught Hameem after school. "I want to go with you to the American woman's school today."

Hameem's eyes narrowed. "Copycat. The first one to do a dare gets points. I already got the ten points for going into her house—you said so yourself."

"I know, I know. But you said she can speak three languages and is willing to give help with our regular studies. I"—Jamal had to swallow his pride. "—could use the help. I'm not as good at numbers as you are. And my French is terrible." That was true—even if it wasn't the *only* reason he wanted to go to Miss Cary's school.

Hameem scratched his head. "Well, I hadn't really planned on going again. I only did it to get points."

"Come on, let's just go see what it's like—no points."

Hameem gave in, and the two boys found themselves once more before the open door of Miss Cary's house. Jamal hesitated, took a breath, then stepped inside. He'd never been inside the home of a Christian before—or a Jew, for that matter, even though a lot of Jews lived in the *mellah,* their own section of Sefrou. The only place the Jews and the Muslims really mixed was in the marketplace.

To his surprise, the house was not that different from his own—but smaller, simpler. A dim passageway opened into a small courtyard, where a handful of other boys Jamal only vaguely recognized sat on the floor around the American woman. Probably from one of the other Islamic schools around Sefrou.

Miss Cary looked up. "*Ahalan.* Hello. *Ma ismok?* What is your name?"

Jamal suddenly felt tongue-tied. He wasn't used to seeing a woman other than his mother without a headscarf and face covering. Miss Cary's hair was brown, like the mud of the riverbank, with streaks of gray and pulled back into a knot at the back of her neck. She wasn't a particularly pretty woman, but her smile was warm and welcoming.

He swallowed. "Jamal Isaam. I—" He didn't know what to say next. He felt very uncomfortable. After all, this was the house of an infidel!

"I am glad you came. Please sit down. I am ready to begin a story—then we will practice our French."

Jamal and Hameem sat.

Miss Cary held up a large picture—the shepherd in the *jellaba* again. Except this time the man was sitting down, with a lot of children crowded around him. "One day," Miss Cary began, "Jesus was walking with His disciples—the men whom He was teaching to carry on His work—when a group of mothers brought their children to Jesus so that He would bless them. But the disciples told them to go away."

Of course, thought Jamal. The mothers and children shouldn't bother a *khatib*—a preacher or teacher.

"But Jesus said, 'Let the children come to me.' And He blessed them. Then He told the disciples that they should have faith like little children."

Jamal poked Hameem and rolled his eyes. Everyone knew that babies like his sisters didn't know anything. It was the old men like Grandfather Hatim who knew everything about faith and God. Miss Cary must have told the story wrong.

But true to her word, Miss Cary drilled the small group of boys on their French verb forms and their vocabulary. At first, Jamal was afraid to answer for fear he would give a wrong answer and get a caning. But when one of the other boys gave a wrong answer, she just simply said, *"Non.* Does anyone else know the right answer?" Realizing that Miss Cary had no cane, Jamal ventured an answer—the correct one—and was rewarded with, *"Bon!* Good! See me after class, and I will give you a picture."

What? She wasn't going to just pass them out? He had earned one, but how would he collect in front of Hameem? He couldn't—not after telling Hameem to get rid of his picture yesterday.

The hour went by quickly. Miss Cary closed her French book. "I must get ready for my next class. . . . *Ma'a el salama,*" she said in Arabic. "Good-bye."

Jamal removed his blue-and-white crocheted cap. *"Ma'a el salama."* He turned to go, casually dropping the cap as he went out.

Outside, Hameem seemed impatient to leave. "Come on. I have had enough school for today. It's almost time for prayers."

"Wait." Jamal felt his thick crop of black hair. "I forgot my cap. I will be right back."

A new group of boys were going into Miss Cary's house—Jewish boys. Did they need help with their schoolwork, too? He slipped in, found his cap, then singled out Miss Cary. "I answered correctly. Could I have a picture, *min fadilak*—please?"

He took the small picture she offered, tucked it into his cap, and pulled the cap tightly down on his head before running out to join Hameem.

Jamal got back home just in time to slip into the mosque in the square for mid-afternoon prayers. A quick glance around located his grandfather and father. As usual, Mirsab Isaam was getting ready to lead the prayers. In row upon row, men and boys kneeled side by side on the prayer rugs, hands on their knees. As his father intoned the first prayer, Jamal lowered his forehead to the ground to the rustling sound of everyone else doing the same. Most Muslim men and boys wore snug-fitting caps that allowed them to do this ritual unhindered. Even the red fez and tassel worn by rich men had no brim, allowing them to bow to the floor in prayer.

Jamal had seen newspaper pictures of European and American men wearing hats with wide brims. How could anyone pray with a hat like that?

As Jamal relaxed in the familiar ritual of the prayers, he felt a little guilty. Had he disqualified himself from the benefits of the fast by attending the infidel's school? In his mind he could hear his teacher listing the five things that were particularly offensive during Ramadan: slander; criticizing someone behind his back *(no problem with those two)*; a false oath *(clear conscience there)*; greed *(hmm, did talking Hameem out of his Jesus picture count as greed?)*; telling a lie *(ouch!— he hadn't actually told a lie, but he wasn't telling the truth about going to the infidel's school.)*

"As-salaam Alaikum." He heard his father give the final blessing. "Peace be upon you." The crowd of men and boys spilled out of the mosque and into the square. Jamal hurried home and immediately ran up to his room. Uncle Samir was nowhere to be seen. Jamal hadn't seen him at the mosque, either. His uncle was a wheelwright by trade and often got called to other towns and villages to repair carts and wagons. He might be gone for days.

Jamal pulled off his cap and fished out the picture postcard he'd put inside. He smoothed the bent edges and looked at the children crowded around the man. Then he noticed something he hadn't seen before: the children were all different colors! Black hair and yellow hair, brown eyes and blue, dark skin and light skin—and every shade in between. Who *were* these children?

He'd have to ask Miss Cary . . . if he went to her school again. His insides tightened—he wasn't sure if it was hunger pangs from fasting or guilt about doing something his parents might not approve of. Should he tell them about the American missionary?

❖ ❖ ❖ ❖

That evening when they broke the day's fast at *iftar,* Uncle Samir was still absent. Good—this was Jamal's chance to say something without his uncle jumping all over him. His mother had made *harira,* a spicy lentil soup with meat, beans, and tomatoes, thick enough to scoop up with the flatbread.

Jamal took a deep breath. "I saw the Americans in the marketplace, too. The woman is a teacher."

His father looked up and frowned. "What kind of teacher?"

"Uh, French, Arabic . . . and numbers. She tutors children who want help before taking their exams."

"Miss Cary? The Christian missionary?" said Jamal's mother, feeding Jasmine, who sat in her lap. "She helped Shu'a Serraj deliver her baby two months ago—I heard the women talking at the river. They said she is very kind."

Jamal stared. He hadn't expected her to be an ally.

Mirsab Isaam looked keenly at his son. "Where did you hear about the American teacher?"

"Hameem told me." That was certainly true.

Jamal's father frowned. "Meddlers," he grumbled. "We can deliver our own babies and teach our own children. Sometimes I think Samir is right. They should take their foreign religion and go home."

Grandfather Hatim chewed thoughtfully. "On the contrary. It strengthens our religion to know what the Christians and Jews believe and how to answer. When I studied Islamic law in Marrakesh, we had many good debates with foreigners. It made us think."

Jamal decided to take the plunge while things were going his way. "I could use the extra help with my studies." He caught the look his father sent his mother; his father was not pleased. But his mother gave a slight shrug and started to clear the table of the nearly empty bowl of *harira*.

Grandfather settled back. "Christians teach many things that are true—about the holiness of God, about loving your fellow man, about the good deeds of Jesus. But you must be alert. They also claim that Jesus was God—how can that be? He was a man. A good man, a saint—but not God's representative. As you know, Jamal, our prophet, the great Mohammed, is the only true representative of God."

Inspired by his grandfather's confidence in him, Jamal blurted, "And the Koran is God's holy word given through our prophet."

Even Jamal's father nodded approvingly. Just then Faheema arrived with the teapot, and Jamal settled back with his cup of sweet mint tea. The conversation turned to other things, but he was satisfied. He had told his family about Miss Cary's school. They hadn't said yes, but they hadn't said no, either. And hadn't his grandfather said it was good to know what the infidels believed so one could make a good argument?

"Jamal! Come on! We're going to watch the Legion do their drills outside the city gates! Some French prisoners are making bricks along the mud banks, too—must be deserters who got caught, poor worms."

Jamal felt torn. It would be fun to run off with Hameem and the other boys—maybe they could even snitch some loot for The Game. But he had been attending Miss Cary's school for over a week now—except for the Friday Holy Day—and even his Islamic teacher seemed surprised at Jamal's new grasp of French verbs.

Not to mention that his collection of the forbidden pictures was growing.

He steeled himself to his resolve and went to Miss Cary's school. He recited all his verbs correctly and got another picture—Jesus standing in a fishing boat surrounded by frightened disciples during a fierce storm. According to Miss Cary, Jesus commanded the storm to stop, and it did. *Hmph*. Maybe Jesus was just braver than His followers.

When Jamal got home, he heard male voices

talking in excited tones in a corner of the courtyard. Uncle Samir was back, along with Mateen and a couple of other friends. The men didn't seem to notice him, so Jamal quickly ran up the courtyard stairs to the second floor balcony. Pulling the small wicker chest from behind his bed cushions and dropping the picture inside, he looked around the sleeping room. He needed a better hiding place for his collection of forbidden treasures—but where? Finally he pushed the chest under the low table that stood along the wall. Uncle Samir wouldn't go looking under there.

But he felt anxious as the family broke the day's fast at *iftar* that night. What if Grandfather or his parents asked him about Miss Cary's school in front of Uncle Samir? But he needn't have worried. Samir's friends had stayed for the meal, and only one thing was on their minds: Abd el-Krim and the rebellion.

"I tell you, Mirsab," Uncle Samir said to his brother, dark eyes gleaming, "we shall see action before the end of Ramadan. Out in the villages, there is talk of nothing else. The Desert Prince has amassed a great army from among all the tribes."

"The French know something is up," Mateen agreed. "The number of troops in Sefrou has doubled."

"*Na'am*—yes. They march and drill outside the city gates every day," Jamal chimed in.

Uncle Samir lowered his voice, as though the walls might have ears, and looked meaningfully at Jamal's father and Grandfather Hatim. "We must be alert. One of these days we will have to choose where we stand—with the infidels . . . or el-Krim."

Chapter 4

The Desert Prince

By the time Jamal got to school the next day—the twenty-second day of Ramadan, or April sixteenth on the Western calendar—reports and rumors were already on the tongues of the farmers and tradesmen coming to sell or buy in Sefrou's markets.

"The Desert Prince has thousands of horsemen, heading toward Fez!"

"They say the French deserter rides with him!"

"Klem? He's not French—even if he did make sergeant in the Legion. Calls himself 'The German Pilgrim,' claims he's a convert to Islam."

"Convert? Huh. Maybe, maybe not. But he knows weapons. Taught el-Krim how to use the guns they captured from the Spanish."

"Ha! No wonder the French want his head!"

Even Jamal's teacher seemed to have el-Krim's rebellion in mind as he drilled them on that day's verse from the Koran again and again: "Sura 61:11— To believe in God and His messenger . . ."

"To believe in God and His messenger . . ." recited the class in unison.

". . . and to fight hard in God's cause with your property and your persons," the teacher intoned.

". . . and to fight hard in God's cause with your property and your persons," the class repeated . . . and on it went, back and forth, through the whole passage.

Later Jamal surprised himself when the teacher called on him to divide two numbers—he was able to do it in his head and he gave the right answer.

Miss Cary's classes were paying off.

Still, he dragged his feet on the way to her street after midday prayers. Uncle Samir had warned that they would have to choose between the infidels (meaning the French occupation) or the rebellion. Miss Cary wasn't French—but it was well known that the American missionaries lived in Moroccan towns under French protection. She didn't have any "idols" in her house—but she told stories from the Christian Bible. Even Grandfather Hatim had said he must be alert to their false claims.

Was he being a traitor to Islam by going to school in Miss Cary's house? He knew Uncle Samir would think so. Maybe he should quit. . . .

Even though his mind felt divided, Jamal's feet took him into Miss Cary's courtyard. After all, he argued with himself, his parents hadn't said no, and his schoolwork was improving. And, he admitted to himself, Miss Cary's class was his only source for the collection of forbidden pictures.

Forbidden. That was part of the excitement of The Game—collecting stuff that belonged to the infidels.

Miss Cary was passing out a small leaflet with Arabic words on both sides, limping as she did so. Jamal had noticed that she limped when she was tired, but when one of the students had asked if she was hurt, she just laughed and called it "the rheumatiz."

"Who would like to start our reading lesson today?" she asked.

Another boy's hand shot up. He stood and began reading. To Jamal's surprise, the reading lesson was about Jesus—a terribly sad story about religious leaders who wanted to kill Him because He claimed to be God's Son—just like God.

Jamal's ears pricked. This was what Grandfather Hatim had warned him about.

Another boy read about Jesus' trial, and still another read how He was sentenced to death by crucifixion—hanging alive on a wooden cross to die a slow, horrible death.

The final reader, however, read that after Jesus was buried, He came alive again on the third day. Jamal's face grew hot. He should not be here listening to this heresy.

Miss Cary held up a large picture of Jesus hanging on the cross. "The death of Jesus was part of

God's plan," she explained. "Our sins keep us away from God, and the punishment for sin is death. But God loved you and me so much that He sent His only Son, Jesus, to earth to take the punishment for our sins. If you ask Jesus to forgive your sins, He will come to live in your heart, and you can go to live forever with God in heaven."

Jamal jumped up. This was blasphemy! "The Koran says there is no God but Allah! The Koran tells us the way to heaven is to pray five times a day, to keep the fast of Ramadan, to take care of the poor, and make a pilgrimage to Mecca at least once in a lifetime. *That* is the way to heaven!"

His eye caught the brazier that kept Miss Cary's pot of water hot at all times. With a burst of self-righteous anger, Jamal thrust his copy of the blasphemous leaflet onto the coals. It burst into flames and the edges curled up. Then he stalked out of Miss Cary's house. He was proud of defending Islam. Uncle Samir would be proud of him, too.

No one came out after him. He looked back inside, where he could hear the rise and fall of Miss Cary's gentle voice. He felt cross. The other boys should have walked out, too. They were Muslims, weren't they? Didn't they know blasphemy when they heard it?

Pacing up and down in front of Miss Cary's house, Jamal told himself he was going to set the other students straight. From time to time he stopped and tried to listen, but all he could hear were boyish voices and occasional laughter. Were they laughing at him? He felt foolish, but he angrily pushed out his chest and stuck his chin into the air. No, *they* were the fools!

With a sudden pang, he also realized he had walked out without getting a copy of the cross picture. Maybe that one was *too* risky, but of all the pictures he had, wouldn't a picture of the infidel Jesus on the cross be worth the most points in The Game?

At the end of the hour, the other boys filtered out of Miss Cary's house. Some of them had a picture postcard in their hands. A few of the boys hesitated when they saw Jamal. "Foolish boys!" he barked, snatching the picture out of one boy's hand. "Don't you know these pictures are blasphemous?" He snatched another picture, and another. "I will get rid of them for you—now go!"

The boys backed off slowly, then turned and ran.

Triumphantly Jamal watched them go. Tucking the pictures into his cloth sash, he ran for home.

Jamal spent the twenty-third day of Ramadan—the weekly Holy Day—with his family and at the mosque. But after school on Saturday, he yelled, "Hameem! Wait for me!"

Hameem, ready to go off with the other boys, raised a skeptical eyebrow. "Aren't you going to the Christian school?" Jamal's daily attendance at Miss Cary's school had been a sore point with his friend.

"No." Jamal gave a shrug. "I got what I wanted."

Hameem grinned. "Good! Come on! We've been

playing war games with the French soldiers when they drill out in the fields—except they don't know it."

Laughing, the boys ran after their friends, but slowed as they picked their way through the basket-weavers' *suq*. The marketplace was abuzz with the latest news:

Abd el-Krim was attacking the string of French outposts between "occupied" Morocco and the western border of Algeria.

"I heard the Desert Prince has captured five, maybe six, of the French forts already!" said a bearded merchant, more interested in talking than selling his stacks of baskets.

"*I* hear he is not taking prisoners." The seller in the next stall winked knowingly.

Jamal eyed Hameem grimly. No doubt the heads of French soldiers were decorating the gates of those forts.

More sober now, the boys threaded their way through the crowded streets and out the city gate. Sefrou in the spring was lush with sprouting olive,

date, and almond
trees fed by the river from the nearby mountains,
swollen from the spring rains. Newly planted fields
of barley and corn were surrounded by large plots of
vegetables and pungent mint plants. Sefrou was one
of the last oases before the stretching desert.

The French Foreign Legion had tramped out their
own parade ground close to the city gates. "Hope you
don't think I've been sitting on my hands while you've
been feeding verbs and numbers into your head,"
said Hameem, giving Jamal a playful shove. "With
all these soldiers running around getting ready to
fight, I've been picking up a *lot* of their stuff for my
collection."

"Like what?" Jamal demanded. Of course it was only fair that Hameem had continued to play The Game—hadn't he been getting points for himself by pocketing Miss Cary's pictures? But was it possible that Hameem had gotten more points than he?

Hameem shook his head. "I'll show you when we *both* show our collections and count points. When?"

Jamal considered. "After Ramadan. How about the first day of Shawwal?"

Shawwal was the tenth month of the Muslim year—only one week away.

"Agreed," said Hameem smugly.

The French Foreign Legion in Sefrou was on high alert. Guards were stationed at the city gates, and other soldiers patrolled the top of the city wall. Reports and rumors continued to feed into the town from camel trains and nomadic Berbers selling sheep's wool: El-Krim had captured nine French outposts; the French had abandoned thirty others and pulled back; overtaken at some of their posts, French soldiers—true to tradition in the Legion—had saved their last bullet for themselves. The latest report—coming right after *Lailat al-Qadr,* the "Night of Power," when Muslims commemorate the night the Holy Koran was revealed to the prophet Mohammed—had tongues wagging at *iftar* in every household in Sefrou:

Abd el-Krim was heading for Taza, only one day's

march from Sefrou.

A new contingent of French soldiers poured into Sefrou. Curious, Jamal followed them as they marched past the mosque just after mid-afternoon prayers. Besides, with only three more days of Ramadan, Jamal had to get more points—*high* points—if he wanted to win The Game.

But as the new soldiers reported for duty at headquarters office, Jamal realized it wouldn't be easy to sneak off with something. Soldiers in blue coats and white pants were *everywhere*. Some were on duty; others waiting for orders. But no one seemed to pay any attention to a mere boy, so he loitered and watched.

A soldier sitting off by himself in the shade of the sleeping quarters caught Jamal's attention. The young man—he couldn't be more than twenty—had a long, angular face and was reading a book. Jamal sidled closer, wondering what the soldier was reading. Then he noticed an empty place on the soldier's uniform where a button was supposed to be. Startled, Jamal stared at the soldier's face.

It was *his* button Jamal had ripped off that day in the basket-weavers' *suq*.

Jamal had an urge to flee. It wouldn't be smart to get caught for thieving! But the soldier's attention seemed diverted by the new arrivals who were going in and out of the sleeping quarters, storing their gear. Jamal saw him shake his head and heard him mutter, "Why don't we just let these people *have* their old town. It's their country, anyway."

Jamal's ears pricked up. The soldier had spoken French, but his accent was Polish or Czech—something eastern European. Jamal shook his head. He never had understood why the French Foreign Legion had so many *foreigners* in it.

One of the recent arrivals stopped abruptly, then took a step or two toward the reading soldier. "I wouldn't say that too loudly if I were you," he whispered sharply. "I've heard what the Legion does to traitors." Then he raised his voice and spoke loudly. "Say, would you show me where I'm supposed to bunk? I don't know my way around yet."

With a friendly nod, the first soldier closed his book, stuck it in his knapsack, and got to his feet. "You sure have a lot of gear," he said, tipping his chin toward a pile of bedrolls and canvas bags.

The new soldier snorted. "Not all mine—my buddy had to go take care of the lieutenant's horse." Just then he caught Jamal observing them. "*Hé, garçon!* Hey, boy! *Parlez-vous Francais?* Come help us take these bags inside."

Not believing his luck, Jamal sprang to life. These soldiers were *taking* him inside! He slung one knapsack over his shoulder and tucked a bedroll under the other arm. Trotting obediently behind the two soldiers, he glanced around him furtively, trying to memorize every detail. The first soldier led the newcomer and Jamal up a set of rough wooden stairs to a large open room, filled with low wooden beds in row after row.

"This is my bunk," said the soldier in French,

throwing the knapsack with his book inside on the military-neat bed. "You can take that empty one there. The way things are going, you'll only be sleeping in it one night."

The other soldier rolled his eyes, then remembered Jamal. "Here, boy. *Merci.*" And he flipped him a coin.

"Merci beaucoup!" Backtracking down the wooden stairs, Jamal hoped he'd remembered the right French words for "thank you very much."

As he came out again into the late afternoon sunshine, his eyes shone with an idea: the book. If he could get the soldier's book right out of his backpack—now *that* was a ten-pointer. Hadn't he seen where the soldier's bed was? But he didn't want to get caught. He'd have to plan very carefully—no, wait. Something the soldier said hinted that the Legion might be leaving for Taza in the morning.

If he wanted to get the book for his collection, he'd have to do it tonight.

Chapter 5

Midnight Raid

Jamal was impatient for the household to blow out their oil lamps and go to sleep. He brought water without being told and poured it into a large brass basin so that his mother could give Jasmine and Jawhara a bath. Then Faheema Isaam swept the wet little girls into the folds of her caftan and disappeared into the "women's rooms" on the second floor.

Grandfather Hatim excused himself soon afterward. Uncle Samir had been strangely quiet and brooding at *iftar* that evening, but he stayed up a long time with Jamal's father, lingering over their mint tea and talking politics and war in low voices.

Jamal checked to make sure that his wicker treasure chest was safely stowed out of sight beneath the low table, then rolled out the soft rugs that served as his bed and lay down. It wasn't unusual to sleep in his loose clothes—no problem there. But what if he fell asleep? Even if he didn't, could he get out of the house without anyone hearing him?

The last light down in the courtyard was blown out, and a moment later Uncle Samir's dark shape appeared in the dim doorway and lay down on his own bed. Jamal didn't move. He waited and listened, hoping to hear the deep, regular breathing—even a snore or two!—that would tell him his uncle had fallen asleep.

Instead, he heard nothing. As though Uncle Samir was lying awake, too.

Well, he'd just have to wait—and not fall asleep, or his golden opportunity would be gone. As he lay there in the dark, Jamal realized he missed going to Miss Cary's house. Her school was so peaceful, and she always had a warm smile and greeting for each of the boys. She didn't seem to have any children or a husband—at least it looked like she lived alone. Did she have a family? Were the American men he saw in the marketplace her brothers? He hadn't seen them since that day he'd pulled off the soldier's button—where had they gone?

Jamal liked the Jesus stories, too—even if He was an infidel. Jesus had been kind to children and lost lambs; He gave food to thousands of people who got hungry while listening to his teachings. The different pictures in the wicker chest floated in his mind—Jesus healing the blind man . . . Jesus healing a little girl . . . Jesus healing a man who couldn't walk. For a man like that—why didn't His followers rise up and fight when His enemies captured and killed Him? Why, Abd el-Krim would—

A rustling noise in the room startled him. Uncle Samir was getting up! Jamal couldn't see in the darkness, but it sounded like his uncle was putting on his *jellaba* and sandals. Sure enough, his uncle's form appeared in the dim light of the open doorway, then Jamal heard soft footsteps going down the courtyard stairs.

Where was he going? Scrambling to his feet, Jamal moved quickly to the wooden railing just outside his room and looked down into the open courtyard. As his eyes adjusted to the muted moonlight, he caught movement disappearing into the passageway that led to the front door.

Uncle Samir was leaving the house!

This was Jamal's chance. Trying to be as quiet as possible, he hurried down the stairs, grabbed a handful of figs from a bowl—at least it was nighttime and he could eat—and silently eased the door open. Poking his head out, Jamal looked up and down the dark, narrow street. His uncle was heading toward the square, the same direction Jamal wanted to go.

Moving as swiftly and quietly as he could, Jamal followed his uncle, keeping to the shadows. A quick glance at the night sky showed a thin cover of clouds, barely letting the glow of the moonlight sift down over the town. Where *was* his uncle going? He seemed to be heading in the same direction Jamal wanted to go—straight to the French garrison.

As they turned onto the last street before reaching the garrison, Jamal saw his uncle pull back into the shadows. Two guards were making their rounds; they passed each other, then continued in opposite directions. Jamal drew closer, stepping into deep doorways along the way, then held his breath until he reached the safety of the next one. Uncle Samir was still standing in the shadows at the end of the street—he seemed to be watching the doorway of the Legion's headquarters.

To Jamal's surprise, a soldier in a French uniform appeared seemingly from out of nowhere. Had he come out of the dark office? He started walking in their direction. Jamal wanted to cry out and warn his uncle—he was going to get caught! But to his amazement, Uncle Samir stepped out of the shadows and met the soldier in the middle of the street.

What was going on? Uncle Samir had no love for the French Foreign Legion. Jamal crept closer, still keeping to the shadows. Now he could see that the soldier wore sergeant's stripes, and his hair and beard were light—probably a "yellow hair." Jamal strained his ears—what were they saying? He couldn't make out any words, but it didn't sound like French *or* Arabic. It almost sounded like one of the Berber dialects that he sometimes heard in the marketplace.

The two men moved farther away. Jamal started to follow, then realized this was his chance to complete his own mission. While his uncle was distracted, he ducked behind the headquarters office and slipped between buildings until he located the soldiers' sleeping quarters. The guards were nowhere to be seen—good. They must still be making their rounds.

Carefully Jamal pushed at the door he'd entered earlier that afternoon. It opened a few inches, just wide enough for the agile twelve-year-old to slip through. Should he leave it open to give him some light? No, the guards on their rounds might notice it.

Moving slowly in the pitch dark, Jamal counted his steps: one, two, three, four, five . . . right. The stairs going to the second floor were right where they should be. Feeling his way up the rough stairway, Jamal climbed. Halfway up, a loud *creeeeeak* protested under his foot. Jamal froze, his heart pounding. But he heard no movement from above or below, so he stepped over the offending stair and continued upward five more steps till he stood at the edge of the large open room.

The room looked different in the dark. What if he couldn't remember where the soldier's bunk was? Again he tried to count the long bumps in the room as he moved between the rows of wooden beds . . . was this the one? Or was it the next?

Uncertain what to do, Jamal hesitated. Some of the dark lumps moved as men grunted and turned over. Snoring started and stopped. He had to act or someone was going to wake up, and he would be caught!

Taking a chance, Jamal moved alongside the bed

he thought he remembered, knelt down, and felt around with his hand. There! A knapsack. But was it the right one? Stealthily he fumbled with the leather straps and buckles. But just as he was about to get it open, the man on the bed turned over and flung out his arm. Jamal flattened himself on the wooden floor in the knick of time, his arms around the knapsack, hardly daring to breathe. Now he was trapped by the soldier's outstretched arm!

But the man's breathing settled into a slow, deep rhythm, so Jamal began fumbling around inside the knapsack. His fingers closed around . . . a book.

Grinning to himself in the darkness, Jamal slowly withdrew the book, then crawled beneath the soldier's arm and hand dangling over the side of the wooden bed. He glanced at the soldier's face—now that his eyes had adjusted to the darkness, he could make out the angular jaw and nose of the book reader. Keeping his body low, he felt his way back toward the stairs, down to the first floor—again stepping over the offending middle step—and poked his head slightly out the door.

No one in sight. He began to breathe easier. Either the guards had not come back this way, or they'd already passed and were gone again.

Giddy with success—oh, how he wished Hameem knew what he was doing!—Jamal tucked the small book into his sash and started to run. He had to get home before Uncle Samir, or he'd be one plucked chicken! Pausing slightly as he came around the small building that housed Legion headquarters, he looked up and down the street. It was empty. Dashing across the open space, he darted into the safety of the shadows—and crashed right into the body of a man he had not seen standing there.

A strong arm grabbed him across the chest and a voice snarled in his ear. *"Sie kleiner spion!"* Panicked, Jamal struggled to free himself. He didn't understand the words—they were neither Arabic nor French—but they sounded sharp and guttural, like German. *Another* foreigner in the Foreign Legion. Twisting to see his captor's face, Jamal recognized the light-colored hair and beard: the French Legionnaire his Uncle Samir had been talking to! At close quarters, the man's face looked familiar . . . where had he seen him before?

Jamal was suddenly aware of a second man standing behind the first. "He's not a spy. *C'est mon neveu*—my nephew." Uncle Samir's voice!

He stopped struggling, but his mouth went dry, and his heart felt like it was pounding in his throat. The sergeant let him go, but Uncle Samir immediately grabbed his arm in an iron grip and marched him down the narrow street away from the garrison.

"What are you doing here?" his uncle hissed in Arabic between clenched teeth. "Why are you spying on me?"

Jamal's feet were flying over the cobblestones as his uncle hustled him along. He licked his dry lips and tried to find his voice. "I—I didn't mean to be spying on you!" he blurted. "I mean—I saw you leave the house, and—and I was curious. So I followed you, but—"

Uncle Samir pulled him up short and shook him roughly. "You followed me? What did you see? What did you hear?"

"N-Nothing, Uncle! I—I—I lost you, so I wandered

around trying to find you, but I gave up and was on my way back home when—when—"

They had reached the edge of the square where the mosque stood. Jamal could barely see his uncle's face in the deep shadows of the tiny street that spilled into the square, but he could feel the tension in his uncle's body relax slightly.

"Hmph." Uncle Samir dropped his grip on Jamal's arm. "Schoolboy prank," he muttered. Then his voice got hard again. "Go on home and keep your mouth shut, and I won't tell your father *this* time—understand? Now go! Go!"

To Jamal's surprise, Uncle Samir gave him a push. Relieved, Jamal ran across the square. He could hardly believe his good fortune! He hadn't planned to tell anyone, anyway. How could he tell on Uncle Samir without telling on himself?

Then a strange thought made him turn around and look back. Uncle Samir had disappeared. Why wasn't Uncle Samir coming, too?

Back inside his own home, Jamal tiptoed into the room the Isaam family used for eating and visiting and felt around on the shelves where his mother stored necessary foodstuffs and supplies. His adventures had made him ravenously hungry, and after being up half the night, he could not count on waking up early in the morning to eat before morning prayers. His probing fingers found what he was look-

62

ing for: leftover flatbread wrapped in a cloth, and a candle and matches.

Back in his room, Jamal lit the candle and set it carefully on the floor before tearing off bites of the flatbread. While still chewing and swallowing, he fished his prize out of his sash: the soldier's book.

Jamal wanted to laugh with glee. What a coup he'd pulled off! He had walked right into the sleeping quarters of the French Foreign Legion *while the men were sleeping* and made off with a book from the personal knapsack of one of the soldiers!

What a rebel soldier he'd make! If his father or grandfather found out, they'd only see it as a foolish, risky game and probably punish him for hoarding stuff belonging to the infidels and desecrating the sacredness of the house. Even Uncle Samir might not understand . . . but Jamal knew one person who would probably praise him: Abd el-Krim, the Desert Prince!

Feeling pleased with himself, Jamal took another bite of bread and turned the book over in his hand to the front cover. He stopped in mid-chew . . . what was this? The words on the front cover were written in Hebrew letters!

He knew it wouldn't be Arabic—few of the ordinary soldiers bothered to learn the language of the country they occupied. But he had expected French— at least he'd hoped so, so he could figure out what the book was about—or maybe the language of whatever eastern-European country the soldier had come from. But Hebrew? Only Jews read or spoke Hebrew. He had no idea what the letters meant, but he recognized the Hebrew writing from signs he saw in the *mellah,* the Jewish section of Sefrou.

He felt confused. An eastern-European Jewish soldier in the French Christian Foreign Legion?

And then he worried. What if it was a Jewish holy book—the Torah? Maybe The Game had gone too far. The button and the canteen and bullet casings he could maybe get away with, even if they did belong to the infidels. But all those Jesus pictures of stories from the Christian Bible, and now maybe a Jewish holy book.

If discovered, Jamal could be in big trouble with his own people.

Chapter 6

The Deserter

It wasn't the call of the *muezzin* that woke Jamal the next morning, but the *tramp, tramp, tramp* of boots on cobblestones in the distance. Jamal bolted upright. The French troops were moving out! This he would like to see!

Dawn had not yet invaded the sleeping room, but as he felt around for his shoes, Jamal realized that Uncle Samir had not returned to his bed. Maybe he had to walk to a distant village to repair a cart wheel. But why didn't he want Jamal to say anything to Father or Grandfather?

Jamal shrugged. What did he care? Right now he wanted to get to the top of the city wall before the call to morning prayer.

Faheema Isaam was already up, lighting the oil lamps and setting out bowls of dates, figs, and almonds for those in the household who arose before the first call to prayer. Only two more days in the month of Ramadan; only two more days of the daily fast. Jamal grabbed a handful of nuts, took a long swig of water from the jug, and scurried out of the house before his mother could ask where he was going so early.

At the end of their narrow street, where it opened into the square, Jamal could hear squads of Legionnaires marching toward the city gates. A few other men and boys spilled out into the gray light of almost-morning, their *jellabas,* caps, and sandals a contrast to the dark jackets, billed hats, and white uniform pants tucked into black boots of the Legionnaires. One of the short figures ran over to him. "I knew you'd come if you heard the soldiers," Hameem half-whispered gleefully.

"We can see better from the wall! Come on!" Jamal led the way as the two boys darted through several streets and alleys to the stairs leading to the top of the wall that encircled Sefrou. They jostled their way through the growing crowd of men and boys who had the same idea and took up a position on the north section of the wall. The sky was beginning to lighten, and they could make out groups of soldiers and officers on horseback heading northeast—toward Taza.

Just then the call of the *muezzin* floated from the top of the minaret of the mosque behind them: "Allah is great! There is no God but Allah!"

But Jamal and Hameem stood transfixed at the sight before them. The soldiers they had heard in the square were the last of the regiment leaving Sefrou. To their surprise, a regiment of cavalry, their horses sleek and champing at their bits, had joined the infantry soldiers who had been staying in Sefrou the past couple of weeks. Had the foot soldiers been waiting to defend Taza until the cavalry had arrived?

Jamal felt a thrill of fear and excitement. Would the French forces hold Taza against Abd el-Krim's desert horsemen? Or would the Desert Prince defeat the French and push them back to Sefrou?

The boys watched until the last company of soldiers had disappeared. By now the sun had started its journey over the horizon and the shadows of night had been exchanged for the muted colors of sandy roads, whitewashed walls, and gray donkeys loaded with bundles of brightly colored cloth and brass and copper.

Jamal and Hameem looked at each other with the same thought: they had both missed morning prayer. Hameem swallowed. "Maybe nobody noticed."

Jamal made a face. "What's the worst that could happen? We might have to make *fidya*." Fidya was compensation for missing or wrongly practicing the required acts of worship. "That's not so bad—we'll just have to donate money or food to the poor."

Hameem shrugged his shoulders gloomily. "Yes, but I will have to ask my parents for the money or food. Then I will have to work it off—double."

Jamal chewed his lip. He was sure to hear about it, too—after all, his father was the *imam* who led the daily prayers. Mirsab Isaam would say Jamal had to be an example to the other boys. But somehow missing morning prayer and having to make *fidya* seemed trifling worries compared to the trouble he *could* be in if his treasure chest was found.

The treasure chest . . . suddenly Jamal remembered. He'd been with Hameem almost an hour already and hadn't told him about his midnight raid at the French garrison. "Hameem! Let's go straight to school—no reason to go home now, anyway. Besides, I have something to tell you on the way!"

Jamal knew Hameem was torn between drop-jaw admiration of his midnight exploit and sheer envy. But when Jamal suggested that the book was worth *twenty* points because of the risk involved, Hameem wouldn't budge. "Ten. That's what we agreed on if we took something from the person of an infidel." All morning long they mouthed words to each other when the teacher's back was turned: *"Twenty." "Ten!" "Come on. Twenty!" "No! Ten."*

The rest of the schoolboys were also abuzz with excitement. The teacher used his cane frequently but couldn't stop the whisperings and restlessness. Finally he gave up and let the boys ask questions. Hands shot up all over the room.

"Are all the French soldiers gone?"

"No. They left two or three platoons to 'guard' Sefrou." The sarcasm wasn't lost on the students.

"Who do you think will win the battle?"

A smile. "We submit to the will of Allah."

"Will the Desert Prince come to Sefrou?"

A pause. "Only Allah knows. But if the rebellion takes Taza . . ." Eyes and ears waited expectantly, but the teacher just said abruptly, "No French lesson today. Let's repeat our verses today from the Koran."

No French lesson? Jamal grinned at Hameem. Even the teacher had his own way of rebelling against the French.

The noontime prayers followed the usual liturgy for Ramadan, but in their hearts, all the boys were praying that Allah would give victory to the Desert Prince.

Sure enough, as the boys came out of school, they saw French soldiers on the walls of Sefrou and stationed at the city gates, and small squads of Legionnaires patrolling the marketplaces. As Jamal and Hameem wandered idly through the basket *suq,* they also saw something else: the two American men were preaching Christianity again.

Instinctively, Jamal glanced toward the old, vacant barbershop, half expecting to see Miss Cary sitting in the doorway, telling stories to a crowd of children. But the door to the shop was closed, half hanging on its hinges. Leaving Hameem in the crowd of Christians, Muslims, and Jews to listen to the lively debate, Jamal wandered over to the barbershop

and peered through a crack in the door. Maybe, just
maybe, Miss Cary had left some of the postcard
pictures behind.

A movement inside startled him and he jumped

back. Then he felt foolish. Probably just a rat! Who was scared of a stupid rat? Sefrou had hundreds of them. He pulled the door open and glanced inside. A piece of paper was lying on the floor halfway back; could it be one of the Jesus pictures? Stepping up into the abandoned shop, he pulled the door shut behind him and headed across the floor. The crack in the door let in a long finger of light, just enough to point him toward the piece of paper.

He grabbed it and held it up to the finger of light. He was right! It *was* one of the Jesus pictures, one he didn't have yet. Could there be more? He crept farther back into the shop, his eyes adjusting to the darkness as he searched the floor.

Thud! Jamal tripped over something and went sprawling. He started to pick himself up, but just then a strong hand shot out and grabbed him. Jamal opened his mouth to yell, but a voice whispered in French, "Shh! Shh! *Je ne vais pas vous blesser!* I'm not going to hurt you!"

Jamal twisted to see who his captor was and found himself staring into the face of the Jewish soldier—the one whose book he had stolen. For a long moment, both the boy and the young soldier stared at each other. Then Jamal tried again to pull free, but the soldier held tight.

"*S'il vous plaît!* Please! I'm not going to hurt you. I'll let you go. Just . . . don't tell anyone I am here."

Jamal's mind was spinning. Had the soldier recognized him last night and followed him to get his book back? But how could he know that Jamal would come by this marketplace and look inside the old, vacant barbershop? And why was he still in Sefrou? Hadn't most of the soldiers marched out into the desert that morning for the battle at Taza?

With sudden clarity, Jamal blurted in French, "You are a deserter!"

"I beg you, do not tell!" whispered the soldier.

Or what? Jamal thought. Would the man report him? It would not be hard to prove—he had the book in his treasure box at his house! The French had brutal ways of dealing with thieves and traitors. But did the soldier know Jamal was the culprit?

Jamal felt the soldier let go of his arm, and before the soldier had time to change his mind, the boy scrambled across the floor of the "vacant" shop and out the lopsided door.

"Oh, there you are!" said Hameem's voice. "I've been looking all over the marketplace for you. What were you doing in that old shop?"

Jamal's heart was pounding, but he tried to shrug casually. "Nothing. Just looked in. Uh, why do you think Miss Cary is not here to tell stories today? Doesn't she usually come to tell stories when the American men preach in the marketplace?"

Hameem shrugged. "I don't know."

"Well, come on. Let's go find out." Jamal walked quickly away from the old barbershop and smiled smugly to himself as Hameem huffed and puffed to keep up with him. At least he had diverted Hameem before his friend had time to ask more questions about why he was in the empty shop.

"Just don't make me late for mid-afternoon prayers," Hameem grumbled as the boys navigated the streets toward Miss Cary's house. "I'll be in enough trouble already for missing morning prayers."

Jamal was having his own doubts. The last time he was at the missionary's house, he had burned her Jesus paper and stomped out of the class. Part of him was still glad he had defended Islam, but part of him regretted what he'd done. She had always been so kind to him, and he would have liked to hear more of the Jesus stories she told.

But now . . . he wasn't likely to find a welcome anymore. He had just about decided to turn back, when he saw a cart piled high with household belongings standing in front of Miss Cary's door.

He stopped, startled. "Look, Hameem. Miss Cary is leaving!"

Hameem's eyebrows shot up. "That is *mosh bikair*—not good. Maybe the French commander doesn't want the Americans in Sefrou if the Desert Prince attacks. Or maybe she's afraid—"

Just then Miss Cary, dressed in her usual pale blue caftan, came limping out of the front door with her arms full of blankets. Catching sight of the boys, she called in Arabic, "Jamal! Hameem!" as she piled the bundle on the cart. "I'm so glad to see you! I was afraid I'd have to leave without telling you good-bye."

Miss Cary's voice was so warm and friendly that Jamal forgot his uneasiness. He ran to the cart. "Where are you going, Miss Cary? Why are you leaving?"

Miss Cary blew a wayward strand of brown hair off her forehead and smiled wearily. "I received a letter saying my elderly parents are very ill. I need to go and take care of them until . . . well, until they don't need me anymore."

"You're going home? To America?"

Miss Cary smiled again, but Jamal did not think she looked very well herself. Sweat beaded her forehead and her hands shook a little. "To America, yes. But Morocco is home to me now." Her eyes got misty. "When I came to Morocco twenty-four years ago, I didn't think I would ever leave. But my parents need me for a little while."

Twenty-four years ago? That was twice as long as Jamal had been alive! "But, why? I mean, why did you come to our country in the first place?"

"Why? Because I wanted to tell the Moroccan people the truth about Jesus. How could I keep such good news to myself?"

Jamal frowned. Truth? Wasn't Christianity just another religion? Grandfather Hatim told him that each religion thought its own beliefs were the "truth," but a person should be loyal to the religion you were born into. He squirmed. Why did he always have such mixed-up feelings when Miss Cary talked about Jesus?

To cover his confusion, he blurted, "Do you need help, Miss Cary? We are strong"—he poked Hameem—"and could load this cart for you."

"*Shokran gazillan,* Jamal—thank you very much." Again Miss Cary warmed him with her smile.

"But I think I need to lie down for a while." Indeed, her pale skin looked even whiter than usual. "Mr. Enyart and Mr. Swanson will be coming along soon to help me after they finish preaching in the market-places. . . ." Her voice trailed off, and a bit unsteadily she walked back into the house. In the doorway, she turned and gave the boys a brief wave of her hand, and then the door closed.

Jamal just stood there, staring at the closed door. Why did he have such an empty feeling? Miss Cary said she was coming back, but . . .

"Jamal?" Hameem was exasperated. "Come *on*! You're going to make me late!" He pulled Jamal back down the street. "I've fasted for twenty-nine days . . . only one day to go," muttered Hameem. "Don't want to lose the good I've gained keeping Ramadan just because *you* want to help an infidel load her lug-gage."

Chapter 7

The Hiding Place

Mirsab Isaam gave Jamal a stern lecture about missing morning prayer that morning and strict orders to stay at home as the family observed the weekly Holy Day that started at sundown that evening. Jamal cast his eyes down respectfully; inwardly he breathed a sigh of relief. It could have been worse.

On Friday—April twenty-fourth on the infidels' calendar; the last day of Ramadan on the Muslim calendar—Jamal obediently accompanied his father and grandfather to the mosque in the square, made up quiet games to entertain his little sisters, and tried not to think about the feast his mother was preparing to celebrate the end of Ramadan. When Jasmine and Jawhara fell asleep for their afternoon naps, Jamal slipped away to the privacy of his sleeping room. But his body and mind were restless. Was the French Foreign Legion deserter still hiding in the vacant barbershop? Surely he would have fled by now! But Jamal desperately wanted to go see for himself.

But that wasn't the only thing that made him feel unsettled. As yet there had been no word from Taza. How had the battle gone? If the Desert Prince gained control of Taza, would he rout the French from Sefrou, too? Everybody seemed to be holding their breath while they waited to hear Taza's fate.

And Uncle Samir . . . he had been gone two days now. Where was he? Why hadn't he come home? Surely he would be home for *Id-al-Fitr,* the three-day Feast of Fast Breaking, which began on the first day of the month of Shawwal. Father and Grandfather acted like nothing was strange about his absence, so maybe Uncle Samir was just doing business in a distant village. But the midnight meeting Jamal had witnessed between his uncle and the light-haired soldier *had* been strange. What did it all mean?

And Miss Cary was going back to America. Jamal didn't know why he felt unhappy to see her go. After all, he'd only known her a few weeks. But she was kind and friendly and had helped him a great deal with his studies. Uncle Samir and his father would probably say, "Good riddance." They called the

Christian missionaries "meddlers." But almost every time Jamal had attended her classes, a woman or child had come to her door for medicine to help a stomachache or cough or fever and often went away with a sack of food, as well.

No more Jesus stories? He had so many questions he wished he'd asked! At least he had the collection of pictures.

After checking the courtyard below to make sure no one was about, Jamal pulled his treasure chest from under the low table and opened the latch. He took out the postcard-sized pictures and spread them all out on the floor. The light in the room was too dim to see well; Jamal jumped up and pulled back the heavy tapestry that covered the one window at the back. Now the light was better.

It was the first time Jamal really had a chance to look at the new picture he'd found on the floor of the barbershop. It looked like the shepherd man—probably Jesus—was cooking fish over a fire beside a lake. Out on the water, several men in a fishing boat were desperately trying to haul in a net crammed full of fish. The net was so full it looked like it was going to break. Some of the men were looking at Jesus, some were looking at the bursting net—but all of them looked astonished.

Curiosity licked the edges of Jamal's thoughts. Why did the men look so surprised? And then he saw something in the picture he hadn't noticed at first: Jesus had wounds—holes—in both hands. Wounds in his hands? Casting a quick eye over the rest of the pictures, Jamal snatched up the picture of Jesus hanging on the cross. Big, fat nails had been hammered through his hands into the wood.

Jamal rocked back on his heels. Oh, how he wished he could ask Miss Cary to tell the story. What was it about? What did it mean?

Uncle Samir still had not returned by *Id-al-Fitr*. But Jamal's mind was fixed on the huge, steaming bowl of *couscous* in the center of the low table. In another bowl, a soup of lamb broth, diced lamb, chickpeas, onions, and spices thickened with beaten eggs, tantalized his nose. Bowls of fresh figs, olives, and dates kept the children's hands busy as they waited their turn to dip into the bowl of couscous with freshly baked flatbread. Sweet fig cakes stuffed with raisins and nuts followed.

Jamal was so full by the end of the meal he wasn't sure he even had room for the sweet mint tea that his mother poured. But if he had hoped to hear news as the men leaned back against the cushions and sipped their tea, he was disappointed. His father and grandfather were strangely lost in thought.

But not Faheema Isaam. Jamal's mother was already hard at work in a frenzy of cleaning the next morning as Jamal pulled on his blue-and-white cap. "Come home right after school," she ordered. "I will have chores for you. Do you understand?"

Jamal sighed. After spending the Friday Holy

Day at home, he had hoped to be free to tally up the points for The Game, which he and Hameem had agreed to do right after Ramadan.

The first day of Shawwal often took on the atmosphere of a festival after the long month of daily fasts. But as Jamal trotted to school, the usual marketplace banter as the merchants set up their stalls was missing. Even the donkeys pulling their carts through the busy streets looked glum. The French soldiers patrolling the walls and the city gates were tight-lipped, their bodies tense, as though they did not know where the enemy would appear—from the desert or within the walls.

But right in the middle of reciting that day's verses from the Koran, the students inside the Islamic school heard the familiar *tramp, tramp, tramp* of soldiers' boots. The boys looked at one another, wide-eyed. Were the French soldiers returning from Taza? What did it mean?

Even the teacher strode to the door of the classroom and looked out. But after only a brief pause, he raised his voice and continued his lesson. "Recite! Sura 64:8: 'So believe in God and His messenger and the light which we have revealed.'"

" 'So believe in God and his messenger and the light which we have revealed,'" murmured a dozen boyish voices.

"What is the 'light' that has been revealed?" the teacher demanded.

"The Koran, our Holy Book!" chorused the boys.

The teacher worked hard to keep the students'

minds on their work, in spite of the sounds that invaded the classroom: boots on cobblestone and waves of murmuring voices and running sandals. Jamal also noted that they had a French lesson that day.

As soon as midday prayer was over, the boys spilled eagerly out into the square, then stopped short as they saw the columns of Legionnaires threading their way into the city, uniforms dirty and torn, faces taut and tired, led by officers on horseback. But not every soldier returned on his own feet. Many lay on litters carried by four soldiers, heads, arms, chests, and legs bound in bloody bandages. And then came the carts carrying the dead.

Jamal knew his mother expected him to come right home, but he dragged his feet, hugging the edges of the crowds of Sefrou citizens to pick up the murmured reports:

"The French managed to hold Taza. . . ."

"But look at the dead and wounded! The battle must have been fierce."

"I heard they lost the element of surprise. Abd el-Krim knew French reinforcements were coming."

"They suspect a spy—from Sefrou—warned the Desert Prince."

"Is the rebellion dead?"

"Far from it, my brother! El-Krim has regrouped and headed for Fez."

"Fez! A royal city!" Ironic laughter. "So! Insignificant Sefrou is safe for the French . . . for now."

Jamal ran the last hundred yards to his door and

scurried inside. By the evening meal, his father and grandfather would have weeded out rumors from real reports. But of this he could be sure: The French Legion had returned, and they weren't running for their lives. His thoughts darted to the old barbershop. If the Jewish soldier really was a deserter, had he managed to get away from Sefrou? If not, what a fool! It would be harder now that the Legion had returned.

"Jamal!" Faheema Isaam swept through the courtyard, which had been scrubbed to a sparkle, and thrust a bundle into his hands. "Nadirah and her daughters already picked up the washing and have taken it to the river. But I forgot my favorite caftans! You must take them to her quickly, or I will have to wait a whole week to wear them again!" Nadirah Serraj had done the Isaam family washing as long as Jamal could remember.

"But I'm so hungry!" Jamal had gone without food during the day for thirty days. He didn't want to miss the noon meal on the very first day of Shawwal.

His mother looked momentarily irritated but then disappeared into the main family room. She quickly rolled up handfuls of spiced, shredded chicken in some soft flatbread, wrapped the rolls in banana leaves, and tucked them into his cloth sash. "And here—take this flask of water. That should keep you." Then she pushed him back out the door with the dresses and head coverings in his arms. "The way you eat, you will soon look like your Uncle Samir!"

Jamal shifted the dirty clothes to one arm and with his free hand unwrapped one of the meat rolls and ate leisurely as he ambled in the general direction of the city gate closest to the river. Then suddenly it occurred to him: He was out! He was free! He could even take a small detour through the basket *suq* to make sure the soldier had gotten away.

The basket sellers were doing a brisk business—almost as if, now that the uncertainty of the battle of Taza was over, Sefrou was in a hurry to get life back to "normal." The din of voices bartering over the price of the woven baskets and the thick crowd gave Jamal good cover as he casually pulled open the door of the old barbershop and stepped up onto the raised floor. The dark, vacant stall stank like a barnyard, but the finger of light from the crack in the door showed nothing, and Jamal was thinking, *Of course he is gone* . . . when a hoarse whisper from the far dark corner made him jump.

"*Vous êtes revenus!*—you came back."

Jamal almost turned and ran. Had the soldier figured out who had stolen his book? But blatant curiosity kept him rooted to the spot. "*Pourquoi?* Why didn't you leave?" he whispered in the best French he could muster.

The dark figure in the corner grunted grimly. "I tried. But it was late at night when the *suq* was finally deserted—and by then the city gates had been locked. And there was no way I could get out during the day—not with this uniform on." The soldier's voice sounded desperate. "*S'il vous plez!* I

need water and food . . . and a place to hide until I can get away."

The soldier was begging! Jamal snorted. "Why should I help you? The French are not my friends."

"Ah! But *I* am your friend." Jamal had to strain to hear the hoarse whisper against the bellowing voices outside. "I do not want to fight your people. I am not even French! I was born in Poland. Joining the Foreign Legion was a big mistake . . . but that's a long story. Please. Do you have water in that leather flask?"

With sudden sympathy, Jamal stepped closer and handed the water flask to the outstretched hand. Fasting from sunup till sundown had been hard enough—but two days *and* nights with no food or water? As an afterthought, he dug into his sash and pulled out the second banana leaf wrapped around the flatbread and chicken.

"Merci!" The soldier hungrily made short work of the bread and chicken and drank thirstily from the leather skin. Jamal's eyes had adjusted to the dim light, and he watched as the soldier ate. His mind was spinning. The soldier wasn't very old—maybe twenty. Should he help him? Even if he wanted to . . . how? And why? Muslims were supposed to help their Muslim brothers, but this soldier was—what? A Jew? From Poland!

Besides, turning in a deserter was worth twenty French francs! That was a lot of money! On the other hand, if he turned him in, would that be helping his enemies? Hadn't el-Krim himself aided a deserter, the infamous Sgt. Klem? But if he didn't turn him in, what would the soldier do if he found out it was Jamal who had stolen his book?

Suddenly Jamal felt like laughing. He had collected and hidden many things belonging to the infidels, but never an infidel *himself*—a deserter. A shiver of danger prickled his skin. That ought to be worth a hundred points in The Game! But . . . how?

His thoughts were interrupted by the hoarse

whisper. *"Quel est votre nom?* What is your name? Mine is David—'Dudzik,' in Poland." The soldier extended his hand. "David Hoffman."

Jamal took the soldier's hand. "Jamal Isaam." Suddenly Jamal looked at his mother's caftans he was carrying. "Here! Put this on." He thrust one of the roomy woman's robes at the slightly built soldier. "And wrap that scarf around your head. You can't stay here. I know where I can hide you."

Uncle Samir was gone. Why couldn't he hide the deserter in his room? No one would think to look for him there!

Chapter 8

Wanted: A Spy

In the thick crowds of the marketplace, no one really noticed the heavily veiled "woman" following Jamal Isaam. At the last minute, Jamal had realized the boots were a dead giveaway and made David Hoffman take them off. He wrapped them in his mother's other caftan, along with the soldier's cap, and told the disguised soldier to carry the bundle, just as any ordinary Sefrou woman might walk through the marketplace with a basket or bundle or child on her hip.

"Do not follow too closely and do not speak," Jamal had warned in a whisper. He wasn't too worried about smuggling the deserter through the crowded marketplace.

And once the soldier was safely stowed away in his room, he would have bought some time to scout out the city gates to see which one was the least heavily guarded. But he hadn't figured out how to handle the biggest problem—getting David Hoffman into his house and up to the second floor. Well, he'd figure that out when he got there.

The unlikely pair waited to leave the old barbershop till Jamal heard the call to mid-afternoon prayer ring out from the top of the mosque's minaret. He set out for home and did not even look to see if the disguised soldier was following him until he reached the corner of his own street. Then he simply held up his hand to signal, "Stay here," and casually walked to the blue door and slipped inside.

"Jamal!" His mother's high voice stopped him in his tracks as he entered the courtyard. "What are you doing back so soon?"

Jamal opened his mouth, then closed it again and swallowed. What should he do now? If he left the deserter out in the street too long, someone might get curious—or suspicious.

"Well, good," his mother rushed on. "I wanted to go to prayer at the mosque, but the girls are asleep and I didn't expect you for another half hour at least. But now you can stay here with them until I get back." Faheema Isaam's voice faded as she disappeared into another room, then reappeared with a long head scarf in her hand, which she wrapped around her head and across her face. "I'm glad you got back sooner—I might stop by the bakers' *suq* and pick up some special bread for tonight's meal. Don't let the girls eat too much when they wake up."

Jamal blinked as his mother sailed out the front door, turned toward the square at the other end of the street, and disappeared.

Then he smiled. He couldn't have planned it better if he'd thought about it all day!

Jamal waited a few minutes, then peeked out the front door. His mother was gone. He looked the other way and saw a figure in a woman's caftan sitting in a doorway several doors down. He beckoned. The figure rose and came swiftly toward him.

The boy put a finger to his mouth and motioned the "woman" inside. Keeping an eye on the door that led into the room where his sisters were sleeping, Jamal quickly led the way across the courtyard, up the stairs to the second-floor balcony, and toward his room.

Just outside the open door, Jamal stopped abruptly in a moment of panic. Behind him, David Hoffman in his stocking feet nearly ran into him. Jamal had been presuming Uncle Samir was still gone—but what if he had returned?

Taking a deep breath, Jamal peered into the room. It was empty.

David Hoffman was exhausted. As soon as he shed the caftan and head covering, the young soldier lay down on Jamal's sleeping rug and fell fast asleep.

But now that he'd gotten the deserter safely into

his room, Jamal realized he still had a host of other problems. What if someone came up to his room? Where could the soldier hide? He pulled the heavy drape over the window, shrouding the room in shadows, and stuffed the soldier's cap and boots on the foot-wide window ledge. *That* would make a good hiding place—as long as no one looked up from the alleyway below.

But he couldn't keep the soldier long. He *had* to get him out of the city tonight or tomorrow at the latest.

Jamal picked up his mother's caftans and long scarves. Should he keep them for the soldier to wear again as a disguise? But what if Nadirah Serraj brought his mother's washing back tomorrow, and the favorite caftans he was supposed to deliver to her were not among them? No, he still had to complete his errand or it would raise too many questions.

As Jamal pondered his options, a plaintive cry from the courtyard sent him scurrying to the balcony railing. Three-year-old Jasmine, dark hair framing her tiny face, stood wailing in the courtyard, crying for her mother. Jamal rushed down the stairs, but within moments, her crying had woken Jawhara, too. Jamal groaned. He had hoped the girls would stay asleep until his mother returned.

The girls' tears, however, stopped immediately when they discovered they'd been left in the care of their big brother. Jasmine begged to be picked up while Jawhara pulled on his shirt. "Take us to the river, Jamal, *min fadilak*—please?" the seven-year-old begged. "You promised!"

"Yes! Yes! The river!" echoed Jasmine, clutching Jamal's neck.

The river? When did he promise to take his little sisters to the river? Probably in a moment of desperation, to get them off his back, he'd said that *someday* he'd take them to play at the river. But not now. He had too many—wait. The *river*? Maybe Nadirah and her daughters were still at the river doing the washing! Now he had a perfect excuse to go again!

He swung Jasmine around and around as she squealed. "Yes! We'll go to the river, little flower—right now!"

Faheema Isaam was busy with the evening meal when Jamal returned with the girls, and she seemed extra pleased that he had taken them off her hands for most of the afternoon. At the riverbank, he had made little boats out of twigs and banana leaves to float at the edge of the river, and his sisters barely noticed as he wandered over to where the mothers and daughters were still scrubbing clothes and hanging them on the bushes to dry. Nadirah Serraj, her head covering fallen loosely about her shoulders after hours of scrubbing clothes on the smooth rocks, had grunted with exasperation when he handed her two more garments to wash, then took them with a shrug. After all, more washing, more money.

Shedding himself of his sisters, Jamal made a quick check on the "visitor" in his room, showed him where the covered chamber pot was located, and agreed together in whispers that David should hide on the window ledge behind the heavy curtain if he heard anyone come close to the room. Then Jamal deliberately spent the rest of the evening downstairs—going to evening prayer, lingering with his father and grandfather after the evening meal, and keeping his ears open.

Id-al-Fitr was normally a festive time. But the Isaam family was not the only family who chose to stay at home and mull over the reports from the battle of Taza. Much of what Jamal had heard on the streets was true: The French had held their control of Taza, but their casualties had been great—greater than the French commander had expected. When the Desert Prince realized that the French had brought in reinforcements to keep their hold on this border town, he had called off his mounted warriors, regrouped, and headed northwest—toward Fez.

Jamal listened patiently with half his attention. The other half toyed with his number one problem: how to get David Hoffman out of his house and out of Sefrou without getting caught. During a lull in the conversation, he asked casually, "When do we expect to see Uncle Samir again?"

His father shot him a sharp look. "Your uncle's business is his own." And that was the end of that.

Finally the oil lamps were blown out and the family retired for the night. Stuffing as much food as he could carry in his wide cloth sash and filling the leather water flask, Jamal finally tiptoed into his room. The room was dark . . . and empty.

"David?"

His whisper seemed to stir the window curtain, and the young Legionnaire slipped back into the room and smiled. "See? Your plan works."

Jamal put a finger to his lips and let his visitor

eat until the household seemed deep in its slumber.

"You said joining the French Foreign Legion was *une erreur*—a mistake," Jamal finally whispered as the shadows in the room deepened into a smooth, velvet darkness. *"Pourquoi?* Why?"

The question seemed to pull a stopper from the young soldier's soul. The words poured out, and Jamal struggled to keep up with the French language and Polish accent.

"I was born in a small village in Poland—surrounded by a lush forest, flocks of sheep and herds of cows, and many gardens. My grandfather lived with us, and he led our family in the many rituals of our Jewish faith. Then came the Great War. I was only seven." David Hoffman swallowed. For a few minutes the young Legionnaire could not continue. Jamal simply waited till he drew a breath and continued.

"During the Great War, my village was destroyed and my family scattered. We did not know what happened to my grandfather. My father took us to Warsaw, but my mother died, and it seemed that all the comforting stitches that had held my young life together had fallen apart, like a ragged quilt."

Jamal listened in the dark in rapt attention. He had never before thought of a French soldier as a child or with a family like his own.

"Then one day my grandfather appeared! He had been searching and searching for us. But he was shocked that my father no longer practiced the Jewish faith, and the older grandchildren—my brothers and sisters—were caught up in parties and friends and cafés. So my grandfather took me under his wing and began to teach me to read the Torah. I loved studying with my grandfather and began to study the Talmud, also. My grandfather began to dream that one day I would become a rabbi."

David Hoffman took a swig of water from the leather flask to wet his dry lips and throat. "But my father was dead set against it. To him religion was worthless. I felt pulled between my father and my grandfather, until I thought I was going crazy. So as soon as I was old enough, I left home. I hardly knew what I believed any more."

"But why the French Foreign Legion?" Jamal asked. "Why Morocco?"

David gave a short, mirthless laugh. "Why, indeed? I thought the excitement of battles might give me the satisfaction I was looking for . . . or maybe I would get killed in battle and bring *some* honor to my family, who thought I was worthless. But joining the Legion was a big mistake." The young soldier shook his head. "It would be one thing to defend my own country from an enemy, but why should I, a son of Poland, fight for the *French* to keep their hold on Morocco, an *African* country? I realized it was crazy!"

Coughing in another part of the house shushed the whispered conversation until all was quiet again.

"How could I go fight against this . . . this man they call the Desert Prince, when it's *his* country? That's when I decided to desert the Legion. Besides," David muttered, "I've heard how the Berber tribesmen cut off the heads of their enemies and stick them on poles. Frankly, I'd like to *keep* my head—at least until I find something worth dying for. I just . . . I just want to go home."

As Jamal digested the soldier's story, he realized he liked this David Hoffman. But this realization tossed his mind in confusion. The deserter was an *infidel*.

Still, he was curious. "If . . . when . . . you get home, will you become a rabbi?"

David shrugged. "I don't know. I feel like my heart is searching for something—something to believe in. A Christian missionary in Fez gave me a Hebrew New Testament—that's the Christian Bible, but written in the Jewish language. I've been reading the stories about Jesus, the one the Christians claim is the Jewish Messiah, or Savior. I've really been thinking about those stories. But . . ." He shrugged sadly, ". . . someone stole it."

Prickles ran up and down Jamal's spine. So *that's* what the book was he had stolen from the soldier's backpack—not a Jewish holy book, but the Christian Bible written in the Jewish language! It was obvious that David did not suspect Jamal as the thief. Should he give it back?

Misunderstanding Jamal's silence, David said ruefully, "So which is the worst sin for a Muslim to hide in his home—a Jew? Or a Christian?"

The next day, Jamal had to wait till after school before he could scout out the French garrison to find out which city gates were guarded. Should he go home first to make sure that the soldier had not been discovered? He decided against it. His mother might easily find something for him to do and keep him from going out again.

Jamal said nothing to Hameem about the deserter he was hiding in his own house—time enough for that when David Hoffman was safely away from Sefrou—but Hameem came along willingly when Jamal said he'd like to hang around the French garrison and find out what was happening.

As the two boys neared the French garrison, they saw a couple of Legionnaires nailing posters to doors, posts, even donkey carts. "Huh," Hameem snorted. "Why do they keep putting those 'Wanted' posters up around here? Do they really think that German deserter, Sgt. Klem, is hanging around Sefrou?"

But something about the posters was different than the ones Jamal had seen before. He sidled closer after the Legionnaires had moved on with their bundle of papers and hammer and nails. The poster was written in French and Arabic, and the words seemed to jump off the paper and hit Jamal between the eyes: "WANTED! Deserter, Traitor, and Spy!" And below that a young, familiar face stared off the paper with a name in bold letters: "Private David Hoffman, 2nd Régiment Étranger d'Infanterie."

Jamal's blood went cold. The French thought *David* was the spy who had tipped off the rebellion that the French were sending extra troops to Taza!

He had to warn David—now!

Chapter 9

Caught!

Leaving a bewildered Hameem hollering, "Jamal! Where are you going?" Jamal took off like a horse heading for its stable. He had to warn David Hoffman! Even more, he had to get the deserter out of his house. What had he been thinking? How stupid he'd been to let The Game go this far!

His feet flew over the uneven cobblestones; his mind raced even faster. David Hoffman, a spy? Impossible! Hadn't he been hiding in the old, vacant barbershop for two days? No way could he have gone to Taza and back by the time Jamal had found him the first time . . . unless—unless he'd gone on the last day of Ramadan, the Friday Holy

Day, when Jamal was unable to go back to see if he was still there.

Now panic forced his breathing into ragged gasps. Jamal had worried that *he* might get in trouble if his family discovered their unwelcome "guest." But if the French found their "spy" in the Isaam household . . .

Jamal rounded the corner of the narrow street he lived on—and nearly collided with two men arguing in heated voices just outside the Isaam home.

"Whoa, whoa, whoa!" barked a familiar voice as a hand shot out and pulled Jamal up short. "What is your hurry, nephew?"

Jamal stared up into the dark, intense eyes. Uncle Samir!

"The galloping colt looks as if he has seen a ghost," smirked Uncle Samir's friend Mateen.

"Go on," said Uncle Samir, giving Jamal a little shove toward the blue door. "Tell your mother I am home and have a guest for the evening meal."

Jamal's heart was pounding with alarm and confusion. On top of everything else, Uncle Samir had come home! Had David already been discovered? No, Uncle Samir would have said something. But instead of hours to get the deserter out of the house, now he had only minutes!

Slipping off his sandals, Jamal scurried barefoot through the passageway, across the courtyard, and up the stairs. Quickly . . . quickly . . . before his mother heard that he was home . . . he had to warn David . . . only a few more steps . . . ah! He'd made it to his doorway—

Jamal stopped short in the doorway and stared. David Hoffman was standing in the middle of the room, holding Jamal's treasure box. The lid was open.

Anger washed over the panic and urgency he'd felt just seconds ago. "Give me my box!" he hissed. "How dare you open it! How dare you touch my—"

The soldier in his rumpled uniform calmly reached into the treasure box and pulled out the small book. "*My* book. So it was *you* . . . *you* are the thief who stole my New Testament." He cocked his head slightly. "Why? Are *you* a Christian?"

Jamal was jolted by the question. "A Christian? Of course not! My family is Muslim! 'There is only one God and Allah is his name and—' "

"I know. 'And Mohammed is his prophet.' " David rummaged in the open box and pulled out some of the Jesus pictures. "Then explain *these*."

In that moment, Jamal forgot he had rushed home to warn David that the French Foreign Legion suspected him of being a spy. Forgot that Uncle Samir was standing outside the house that very minute and likely to come up to the sleeping room shortly. "Give me that box!" he snapped, grabbing for the wicker treasure chest.

He had expected David to resist. But as he grabbed, the box suddenly flew out of both their hands and went crashing to the floor. The contents spilled all over the rug, and some of the items—the shell casings, the pocket comb, the button—bounced off the rug, skittered out the door onto the balcony, and dropped down into the courtyard below.

"What is that?" yelled a voice from below, followed by loud thumps as heavy feet took the stairs two at a time. Sheer panic rooted Jamal to the spot where he stood, and the next moment Uncle Samir loomed large in the doorway. But his eyes only focused on Jamal, then at the pictures scattered on the floor, and back at Jamal.

His heart pounding, Jamal turned his head slightly and took in the room at a glance. David was gone! But where? The window?

"Where did these come from?" Uncle Samir spit out the words, pointing at the pictures. "These have nothing to do with Islam! These are pictures from the infidel Bible. Are these yours, Jamal? You—you have blasphemed our house to bring them here! You—"

"*Ils sont les miens.* They are mine."

To Jamal's shock, David Hoffman stepped from behind the heavy tapestry that covered the back window of the room. He knelt on the floor and began to pick up the pictures. Jamal was speechless. David was giving him an excuse! But . . . but why?

Uncle Samir's face had turned purple with rage. "What are you doing in this house, you arrogant infidel?" His hand moved to the knife he wore in his cloth belt under his *jellaba.*

"*Pardonnez-moi.* Forgive me. I did not mean to desecrate your home. I . . . was hiding. The boy caught me, and in my haste to get away, I stumbled over this box and dropped my pictures." David gathered up the last of the pictures and stuffed them in the pocket of his shirt under his uniform. "I will go now."

Uncle Samir drew out his knife. "Not by that window you won't." Roughly grabbing the front of the young soldier's uniform jacket, the big man yanked David toward the doorway. What was his uncle going to do? For a brief instant, Jamal's hopes rose. Maybe he was just going to throw him out into the street.

But as they reached the balcony and the daylight

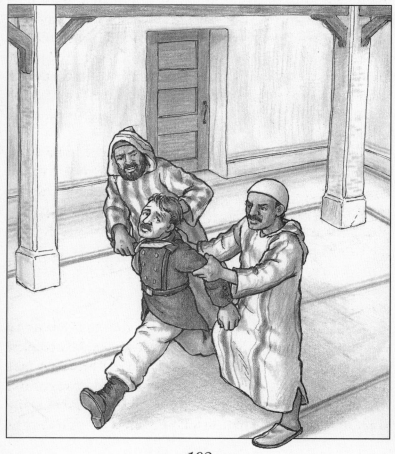

from the open courtyard, the big man suddenly stopped and peered closely at the soldier's pale face. "Wait! I have seen your face—yes! On the new poster! Ha, ha, ha, ha!" Uncle Samir's laughter startled Jamal.

"The French deserter, are you? Ha, ha, ha, ha!"

A sly smile played on the big man's face. "The French commander is looking for you. Ha, ha . . . your fate is just what you deserve." With a quick move, Samir pressed the knife to David's neck and pushed him out of the room and down the stairs.

Jamal still stood rooted to the spot. He was off the hook. His uncle believed David! But he hadn't told David that the French suspected him to be a spy—a traitor! The French executed spies and traitors! Would David have risked getting caught if he'd known?

Jamal rushed to the balcony that overlooked the courtyard below. Mateen had a grip on David's other arm, and Jamal's uncle was still laughing—a dark, gleeful laugh. "Maybe I should thank you, foreign pig. Once they have *you*, they will not keep looking for their spy. Ha, ha, ha, ha, ha!"

As the front door closed, Jamal scurried down the stairs and gathered up his fallen treasures. But back in his room, the implications of Uncle Samir's last words settled on Jamal like sand after a desert dust storm. It couldn't be! Uncle Samir . . . was *he* the spy who had warned the Desert Prince? So! That was what he was doing at the garrison that night! That was why he had disappeared for the past few days!

Jamal's legs suddenly felt like cooked noodles. He sank down onto the floor and aimlessly began putting the items he had collected for The Game back into his treasure box. But it felt strangely empty without the pictures.

His emotions fought with each other. Relief that he had not gotten into trouble with Uncle Samir mixed with anger that David Hoffman had taken his Jesus pictures. Was David paying him back for stealing his book? The book was gone, too—David must have slipped it into his pocket, as well. Jamal could hardly complain about the soldier taking his own book. But the pictures—they were *his*, fair and square. Miss Cary had given them to him—he hadn't even stolen them. Even though she'd given them out to other boys, he was sure no one had kept more than one or two. He had made sure of that, darkly hinting that it would be blasphemy to keep them. But even if they had, surely no one had a whole collection of Bible pictures like his.

Under the relief and anger, another feeling rose to the surface—a sense of loss. The pictures had come to mean a great deal to Jamal. He had liked to spread them out on the floor and look at them, recalling the Jesus stories he'd heard from Miss Cary. There was something about Jesus, the things he said and the way he made people feel loved and important, that made Jamal hungry to know more. But now even the pictures and the stories they represented were gone.

And so was David . . . the enemy who had become his friend.

Shaking himself, Jamal jumped to his feet, casting about for his sandals. Where had Uncle Samir taken the deserter? To the French garrison, no doubt. But what was going to happen to him? He had to find out!

Once more Jamal's feet flew over the cobblestone streets of Sefrou, past the square and the mosque, through the rest of the Muslim section of the town, and finally to the clump of sun-baked buildings that had been taken over as French headquarters. Stepping into a doorway where he had a view of the main quarters, Jamal searched vainly for some sign of his uncle or David Hoffman. There were a good many Legionnaires standing about, some stiffly on guard outside the headquarters, others looking this way and that and talking to one another in anxious tones as if something had just happened.

As Jamal watched from the shadows, the door of the headquarters office was flung open and two armed guards marched out, followed by two more— with David Hoffman between them. Jamal's throat tightened. The young Polish soldier shuffled along as best he could in the leg irons that circled his ankles where his boots had been, his hands bound behind him. His jacket was gone; all he wore was a shirt and his pants.

Another man—a colonel—appeared in the door-way. "Take him to the stockade!" the officer roared. "He won't be there long!" His eyes roamed over the other Legionnaires who had gathered to stare at the prisoner as he was led away. "Watch and learn what the French Foreign Legion thinks about spies and traitors!"

Chapter 10

The Dilemma

Faheema Isaam had heard the commotion as Uncle Samir and Mateen dragged the deserter out of the house that afternoon, and peppered her brother-in-law with questions that evening. "How did that infidel get in this house? Why did he come here? What if you hadn't caught him, Samir? Why, he might have killed Jamal—or all of us!"

Jamal dipped his bread into the spicy food in the middle of the low table and listened as his uncle answered with brief, almost impatient, replies. Once or twice he gave a hard look at Jamal, as if telling him to do the same.

Grandfather Hatim and Jamal's father took the news as just an unfortunate incident that ended well. "Now, nothing serious happened, Faheema," chided her husband. "No use worrying about something that's over and done."

Over and done? Jamal stuffed more bread into his mouth, even though he wasn't very hungry. It wasn't over and done—not for David Hoffman.

Jamal excused himself from evening prayers and went to bed early, but he could not sleep. He was still awake when Uncle Samir came into the room with a candle, got ready for sleep, then blew it out. He was still awake when his uncle's steady snores punctuated the darkness.

What was going to happen to David Hoffman? Just the night before, in this very room, David had been telling him about his family and boyhood in Poland . . . that he didn't want to fight for the French to keep Morocco, how he just wanted to go home.

Now he was in prison for deserting . . . and even worse, they thought he was a traitor and a spy.

The French Foreign Legion was tough. Some soldiers thrived on the discipline and comradeship that made brothers out of men from diverse backgrounds and countries. In the Legion, a variety of adventurers, misfits, and even former criminals found a career. But desertion was common—and the Legion was hard on those it caught. Jamal remembered the soldiers he'd seen outside the walls of Sefrou, stripped of their weapons and uniforms, making bricks in the hot sun under the sharp eyes of guards. It was common knowledge that deserters were expected to make one thousand bricks a day—and if they failed to meet their quota, they got no food that night back in the stockade.

Jamal kicked off his blanket and sat up, sweating. If the French officers thought David was a spy, he would not be making bricks. They'd put him in front of a firing squad.

But he wasn't a spy! Jamal had seen him the same day the French marched for Taza—he couldn't have gotten there and back. But if Jamal admitted that he knew where David had been for the past few days, he would be admitting that he had hidden him. That would get him in big trouble. And even if he told, would anyone believe him? He couldn't prove David wasn't a spy—unless Jamal told what he suspected about his uncle.

Jamal's clothes were soaked in sweat. Getting up quietly, so as not to waken his uncle, Jamal pushed aside the heavy curtain hanging in front of the window and sat on the wide ledge, trying to cool off.

This was where David had been sitting when Uncle Samir came rushing into the room just a few hours earlier. He could have stayed behind the curtain and maybe never been discovered. But David had risked his freedom to come to Jamal's aid. Now David was going to die for it!

But Jamal knew the truth. What was *he* willing to risk for the truth?

The next morning, the third day of Shawwal, the

school was once again abuzz with news coming into the town with merchants and travelers. Abd el-Krim and his mounted horsemen were camped outside the gates of Fez. Would there be a battle? Would Fez, one of the royal cities, fall into the hands of the Desert Prince? Or would el-Krim be pushed back into the desert once and for all?

But Jamal, tired and irritable from his sleepless night, sat woodenly on his bench, hardly hearing the whispers around him. He felt caught in a web, like the flies that twisted and turned in the gauzy nets spun by Sefrou's large spiders in the corners of the room.

After school, he just glared at Hameem when he demanded to know why Jamal had run off without a word the previous afternoon. Hunching his shoulders, Jamal wandered aimlessly through the various markets. What should he do? How did he get himself into this mess?

"In the name of Allah!" whined a beggar, thrusting a tin cup under his nose. Jamal just brushed past and kept on walking. "Curses on you, then!" shouted the beggar after him.

Maybe he was already cursed. Everything was going wrong.

Looking up, Jamal realized he'd wandered into the French military quarters. And he realized what he wanted to do. He wanted to see David Hoffman. He had to talk to him!

Taking off his cap—he'd seen the French do this when they wanted to show respect—he cautiously opened the door of the headquarters office. The man at the desk barely looked up. "Hmph?"

Jamal swallowed. His mouth and throat were dry. French, he had to speak French. "Could I see *le prisonnier* . . . uh, David Hoffman?"

This time the man looked up. "*Pourquoi?* Why?" He didn't wait for an answer. "No one is allowed to see the prisoner."

Jamal crammed his cap back onto his head and backed out of the office. "Hey!" shouted a voice. "Watch where you're going."

Jamal jerked his head around to see a frowning lieutenant trying to come in the door he was backing out of. "*Excusez-moi,*" he mumbled.

The lieutenant's boots thumped on the wooden floor as he went inside. "The colonel wants to see me?" he asked the man at the desk. He pushed the door shut, but not before Jamal heard the other man say, "Yes. He wants you to handpick the men for the firing squad."

A cold hand seemed to clutch Jamal's heart. The firing squad! Now he was more determined than ever. He *had* to see David Hoffman. And he had an idea that might work!

Immediately after mid-afternoon prayers, Jamal asked his mother if he could prepare a basket of food. Faheema Isaam looked puzzled. "Why?"

"For the prisoner." He said it simply, but his

thoughts were anything but matter-of-fact. Why had he asked his mother for the food? What if she said no? He could have managed to sneak some food out of the house. And why did he tell her whom it was for? His mother had been very upset to learn that an infidel had been hiding in her own house!

But he was tired . . . tired of weaving a web of lies and half-truths and secret plans. He hadn't really thought about what to say. The truth just came out.

Faheema Isaam took her son's chin in her hand and lifted it, looking deep into his eyes. He looked back at her, unblinking. They stood that way for a long moment, then she dropped her hand. She seemed satisfied. "Take whatever you want—just don't take the fresh chicken I'm soaking for supper tonight."

Surprised, Jamal lost no time packing a small basket with flatbread, cold meat wrapped in banana leaves, pomegranates and tangerines from the fruit bowl, and some almonds. He wasn't sure his idea was going to work, but it was worth a try. When a local citizen got arrested, he only got fed if his family brought food on a daily basis to the jail. The Legion probably fed its own prisoners—but maybe the guards wouldn't care who brought it.

Jamal's many scouting expeditions to the French garrison with Hameem paid off as he skirted the headquarters office and headed for the squat building he knew held the stockade. He walked among the throngs of Legionnaires as if he had business there, and no one questioned him. As he expected, a guard leaned against the wall next to the door of the stock-ade, holding his rifle at ease.

"What do you want?" The guard's voice was mostly bored.

"Food for *le prisonnier*—Private David Hoffman." Jamal tried to say it matter-of-factly, even though his heart was racing.

"Food? All right. I'll send it in." He took the basket from Jamal. "Poor devil," the guard muttered as he disappeared inside.

The moment the guard's back was turned, Jamal scurried out of sight around the side of the building, then crept along the wall until he got to the back corner. What if they had guards stationed at the back, too? But the tiny alley at the back of the stockade was empty. Guess the French weren't worried that the Desert Prince would come to rescue *this* deserter. The rebellion had already moved their forces and laid siege to Fez.

"Hey! Hoffman! Somebody brought you some food!"

Jamal's ears pricked up. He could hear the words clearly. But which barred window? He hunched over and crept beneath the first window, then the second. Talk, somebody, talk!

"Food? For me?" That was David's voice. "Who brought it?"

"*Un garçon*—a boy. Can't open the door, but I'll hand the stuff through the bars."

Aha! The voices were coming from the third window. Hardly daring to breathe, Jamal waited until he thought he heard the guard moving away. Then he waited another long minute. He was just about to risk raising his head and looking in when he heard a low voice right above him.

"Jamal?" David's voice!

Jamal rose from his crouch to see David Hoffman's face peering out through the bars of the window. A smile creased the young man's face as the boy's head popped into view.

"I *knew* it must have been you who brought the food! Who else would—"

"*Pourquoi,* David?" The words tumbled out of Jamal's mouth as if they would no longer remain bottled up inside him. He had no time for chitchat. He had to know. "Why did you risk getting caught just for me?"

David Hoffman was quiet for a moment, then disappeared from the window. A moment later he was back and pushed a stack of postcard-sized pictures through the bars. They were Jamal's Jesus pictures. David tapped the one on the top. "That's why."

Jamal took the pictures and stared at the one on top. It was the picture of Jesus hanging by nails in His hands on a rough cross of wood. He looked up at David. He didn't understand.

The prisoner shrugged. "You hid me when I asked for help; you gave me food when I was hungry. I couldn't let you get in trouble on my account."

"But they think you are the spy, the traitor who warned el-Krim!" Didn't David realize that the trouble *he* was in was ten times worse than anything he'd saved Jamal from?

David gave a little snort. "Almost funny, isn't it? They think I'm guilty of daring exploits, and I'm just a homesick coward."

Jamal shook his head. "You are not a coward. You let yourself get caught to keep me out of trouble."

David's eyes were surprisingly calm. "It doesn't matter. Maybe that's the one good thing I've done with my life. And that's not very much compared to what He did." David pointed to the picture.

Jamal was confused. "What do you mean?"

David beckoned Jamal closer, and the boy and the prisoner bent their heads as close as the barred window would allow. "I had started to read the Hebrew New Testament the missionaries gave me before you . . . um, took it."

Jamal felt his face flush. *Stole* it was more like it. He was nothing but a thief.

"But last night in my cell," David went on, "I started to look at some of the pictures that I kept from your treasure box. And I recognized some of them as stories that I'd read in the New Testament: Jesus as a boy talking to the religious elders in the temple . . . Jesus commanding the storm to be still . . . Jesus healing the blind man . . ."

But, David said, even though he had seen the crucifix in the garrison chapel and vaguely heard Christians refer to Jesus dying on a cross, he'd never read the whole story. "So last night, sitting in this jail cell, I read the story of Jesus' death and resurrection."

"Resurrection!" Jamal hadn't ever heard that word. "What do you mean?"

"Wait a minute. I'm not there yet." David almost seemed to be reasoning with himself. "Even non-Christians admit Jesus was a good man. And *He* claimed to be the Son of God—yet He let himself be killed as a common criminal. If He was God, why didn't He even try to defend himself? And they crucified Him along with two common thieves. One thief made fun of Him, but the other one expressed sorrow for his crimes—like he was asking Jesus to forgive him."

David paused, as if digesting his own story. Jamal kept silent, willing his new friend to go on. Finally David said, "Not only that, but hanging there on that cross, Jesus asked God—called Him 'Father'!—to forgive the people who wanted Him dead."

David's voice got husky. "I couldn't understand that kind of love—willing to forgive the very people who kill you? But during the night, I had a dream— oh, Jamal! It was so real, like a vision. Jesus was standing in my jail cell, and He showed me the nail scars in His hands. 'I did it for you, David,' He said. 'I did it for you.'"

David turned his head away from the window and listened. Jamal strained to hear, too, and heard the sounds of voices and footsteps within the stockade. The young prisoner looked back and smiled at Jamal. "You better go, my friend." He didn't seem afraid. "Don't worry about me, Jamal. It's going to be all right now."

The voices from within grew louder, and David disappeared from the window. Jamal stumbled away, his pictures once more hidden in his cloth belt. But his mind was screaming, *No, no! It isn't all right!*

Chapter 11

Facing the Truth

Jamal felt more mixed up than ever. He wanted to burst into Legion headquarters and make them listen to him. David Hoffman wasn't a spy! But how could he do that without casting suspicion on Uncle Samir, or getting himself—and maybe the rest of his family—in serious trouble for hiding a deserter? Whose side was he on, anyway—Morocco's French "protectors"? Or his own people?

Unsure what to do, Jamal stumbled out of the military compound and wandered aimlessly through the streets of Sefrou. The Game seemed so unimportant now. He scarcely noticed the pungent smell of saffron and garlic and the sweet smell of cinnamon and mint as he pushed his way through the crowded *suq* that sold spices. The din of voices hawking their wares, chickens protesting in their wire cages, and the jangle of bells the beggars used to attract attention became a mere background to his own confused thoughts.

He wished he could talk with someone—but who? Not Uncle Samir! . . . even though his uncle probably knew more than anyone the truth of the matter.

His father? Mirsab Isaam was a smart man who knew how to get along in a fractured society and refused to dwell on injustice and anger like his brother, Samir. He was happiest when his children did what they were told and caused no grief that kept him from his responsibilities as *imam*.

No, no, his father would not understand. And even though it had been several years since Jamal had tasted the end of a leather strap, his father might not think him too old yet for a thrashing.

Grandfather Hatim? Maybe. The old man was wise *and* patient, willing to listen. But even his grandfather would be shocked that Jamal had deliberately brought an infidel into their home. Jamal knew his grandfather loved him—but he loved Islam more.

His mother? The way she had looked at him when he asked for the food . . . did she know in her heart? But Jamal knew his mother would be hurt by the confusion and questions that plagued him. She only wanted her family to live in peace, to keep the traditions of their faith.

Hameem? Ha. Hameem was no smarter than he was.

Suddenly Jamal went sprawling. "Watch where you're going, boy!" yelled a voice above him. Jamal scrambled out of the way to avoid being trampled by the camel and driver he had just run into, then spit out the gritty dirt in his mouth and surveyed the raw scrapes on his hands. He needed someplace safer to think!

Jamal ducked out of the crowded market into a quieter street, then stopped abruptly. Miss Cary's street! Why had he come this way? Well, he might as well turn back. The missionary teacher was gone now—

Just then, the familiar door opened, and a woman in a blue caftan with a black scarf draped around her head stepped out of her house. Jamal's mouth dropped in astonishment. It couldn't be . . . but as he watched the woman place a box tied with rope into a pushcart, then straighten with a hand on her hip as if it hurt, he was sure. The woman was Miss Cary herself!

"Miss Cary!" Spurred by this discovery, Jamal ran toward her open doorway. "Miss Cary!"

The American woman, shielding her eyes against the bright afternoon sun, broke into a smile. "Jamal Isaam! My goodness! Didn't we already say good-bye?" she teased in Arabic.

"Yes, but . . . why are you still here? I thought you were going back to America!"

"I am, I am." She laughed ruefully. "But I came

down with another case of Malta fever and had to go to bed. Better now—but I still had a few last-minute things to pack. Sure could use a cup of tea, though. How about you?"

Jamal nodded eagerly. Ramadan was over—he could drink tea with Miss Cary with a clear conscience. But he didn't really care about tea. Running into Miss Cary felt strangely like being thrown a rope after falling into the river. Could he . . .? Would she . . .?

He watched as she scooped mint tea into a tall teapot, then poured hot water over the fragrant leaves and let them steep. She didn't speak, just moved comfortably about the nearly empty room, setting out two small cups, a spoon, and a small bowl of sugar cones on top of a box.

As Miss Cary sipped her hot tea, the quietness between them was like an invitation, and Jamal found himself telling her everything that had happened in the past few weeks. He blurted out the whole story—about The Game he and Hameem had made up to defy the infidels by collecting their personal stuff . . . about his collection of Jesus pictures . . . about always looking for something more risky and exciting to earn more points.

Jamal watched Miss Cary closely when he told her he had come to her school primarily to collect the infidel pictures to get points for his game. Her eyebrows went up, but she didn't seem angry. So he took a big breath and told her about stealing David Hoffman's Hebrew New Testament the same night he ran into his uncle on a mysterious midnight errand. Then discovering David had deserted when the Legion marched to Taza ... hiding the deserter in his room ... David getting himself caught to protect Jamal when Uncle Samir found the pictures.

"Now David has been condemned as a traitor and a spy! But I *know* he can't be the spy they're looking for, and ... and I think my uncle knows it, too."

Jamal stopped and gulped. He couldn't say what he thought, that the real spy might be his uncle! He stared miserably at his toes, his untouched tea getting cold in its cup.

Miss Cary nodded thoughtfully but let the silence stretch once more between them. She poured herself another cup of tea and sipped it, her gentle eyes watching him.

That wasn't all that was on Jamal's mind—something he'd wanted to ask Miss Cary but thought he'd missed his chance. "Miss Cary, what did David mean about the picture? About Jesus saying, 'I did it for you'?"

"Ah!" Miss Cary seemed to come alive. Setting down her teacup, she rummaged in a big cloth bag and pulled out her own well-worn Bible and some Scripture portions written in Arabic. "Long ago, in the days of Abraham and Moses," she explained, "God gave mankind rules to live by. But again and again people turned their backs on God and disobeyed His laws."

Jamal nodded. He knew how difficult it was to keep all the rules of Islam.

"God is holy, but sin is the opposite of holy. Obedience to God leads to life, but sin leads to death."

Again Jamal nodded. This was true in Islam, too.

"In Old Testament times, people who wanted to ask God to forgive their sins sacrificed a perfect lamb or other animal that had no blemishes. Something had to die to pay the penalty for sin. But God had an even greater plan—to send His own Son, Jesus, to earth to become the ultimate sacrifice for our sin. Here—read this from the New Testament."

Miss Cary handed Jamal some Bible verses written in Arabic. He read the one she pointed to: " 'For God so loved the world, that he gave his only begotten Son, that whosoever believeth in him should not perish, but have everlasting life.' "

Miss Cary smiled. "See? That's what your friend David Hoffman realized—that Jesus died on the cross for *his* sins."

Jamal's eyebrows came together in a frown. He had always been taught that a Muslim must earn a place in heaven by faithfully keeping the five basic tenets of Islam: declaring that Allah is God; prayer five times a day; observing the fast of Ramadan; giving to the poor; and making a pilgrimage to Mecca. How could someone else do it for you?

As if in answer to his own question, he remembered asking David outside his cell window why he'd let himself get caught just to protect Jamal from the consequences of his own actions. That was like . . . why, that was like—

"Did you say David Hoffman was reading a *Hebrew* New Testament?" Miss Cary's question interrupted Jamal's thoughts. "Hmm. If, as you say, David was taught the Jewish faith by his grandfather, he must have known the ancient prophesies of a Messiah who would come to save all people." She leaned close to Jamal and gazed into his eyes. "Jesus is that Messiah, Jamal, the Lamb of God. And He paid the death penalty for all of our sins—yours, mine,

David's—so that whoever believes can live in heaven with our holy God when we die."

Jamal was so startled by what Miss Cary was saying that he nearly fell off the stool he was sitting on. All his life, he had thought that Jews and Christians and Muslims had nothing in common—that everyone who did not follow Islam was an infidel, even if all three religions did share Abraham as a common ancestor. But could the promises God gave to Abraham really be meant for *all* of them? If Jesus was the promised Messiah . . .

This was too complicated for Jamal! A more immediate problem pressed on his mind. "But what about David *now*? He isn't a *spy*. But if I tell what I know, I will be speaking against my own uncle. My own family!"

Miss Cary nodded in sympathy. "You are a bright boy, Jamal. What does the Koran say about speaking the truth?"

The missionary teacher stood and started to load the last of her things into the pushcart outside the front door. Jamal followed her, thinking about all the Koranic verses drilled into him in school. No doubt about it. A "good" Muslim should be honest and upright—something he had failed at miserably of late.

Hot tears suddenly blinded Jamal's eyes. Embarrassed, he turned his back to Miss Cary and pretended to retie a rope around one of the boxes in the cart. He had fooled himself into thinking he'd only been playing a game—but it had led him to steal and lie and . . .

He felt Miss Cary's gentle hand on his shoulder. "Jamal, look at me."

Jamal swiped his eyes and nose with the back of his shirt-sleeve and turned around slowly, still staring at his toes. But Miss Cary tilted his chin up.

"Jamal, all the great religions teach their followers to be truthful. But Jesus *is* Truth." Miss Cary dug in the cloth bag again and pulled out her Bible. "In John's Gospel, chapter 14, verse 6, Jesus said, 'I am the Way, the Truth, and the Life. No man cometh unto the Father, but by me.'" She smiled, a hint of sadness in her eyes. "That's why I came to Morocco, Jamal, to share that Good News. If you remember nothing else I've taught you, remember that."

Miss Cary stuffed her Bible back into the cloth bag and added it to the boxes and bundles on the pushcart. "There! That's that. There's a truck waiting for me outside the city; will you help me get this old cart to the south gate, Jamal? I'm heading for Casablanca tonight." She chuckled with good humor. "I hear Fez isn't exactly a safe haven for 'infidels' these days."

Jamal gladly grabbed the handle of the pushcart and pulled it behind him while Miss Cary steadied the load. As the cart rumbled through Sefrou's rough cobblestone streets, a parade of children began to collect behind them, both Muslim and Jewish, calling, "Good-bye, Miss Cary! Good-bye!"

Sure enough, an ancient truck, covered with a thin coat of grimy sand, stood waiting outside the south gate, its driver asleep in the shade of the undercarriage. But with a little prodding and an extra coin, he crawled out to load Miss Cary's things into the back of the truck while she clambered into the cab.

"Good-bye! Good-bye!" The gaggle of children waved and waved as the truck headed south toward Casablanca in a cloud of dust. But Jamal was already running back through the gate as fast as his legs would take him.

He had to get to the French garrison! He wasn't sure what he was going to do, but he had to do *something* before it was too late!

Chapter 12

He Did It For Me

Jamal knocked on the door of the French Foreign Legion office, his knees trembling. What was he going to say? He glanced up at the sky and realized the sun had dipped below the western horizon. Had he already missed evening prayers? He couldn't remember even hearing the call of the *muezzin*. His mother would be worried if he didn't show up for the evening meal.

Why wasn't anybody answering? Jamal knocked again, harder this time. He heard a chair scraping and boots on the wooden floor, then the door jerked open. "You again?" The man he'd seen behind the desk earlier that day had a napkin tucked in his shirt collar and bits of beef hanging from his mustache.

"I—I need to see the colonel." Jamal had no idea who "the colonel" was, but that's who the lieutenant that had come in behind him had asked to see.

"Colonel Maire is eating his dinner. Go away." The man started to close the door.

"No! Wait!" Jamal stuck his foot in the door. "I have information about the—the accused spy, David Hoffman. It's urgent."

The man's beady eyes locked on Jamal. "What information?"

Jamal willed his knees to stop shaking. "My information is for the colonel's ears only—and he'd be mighty upset if you kept me from seeing him," he said with more confidence than he felt.

"Hmph." The soldier hesitated. "Wait here."

Shadows were filling the surrounding streets and oil lamps lit first one window, then another, and another, with thick yellow light. After a few moments, the man with the napkin at his neck reappeared. "Come along."

Jamal followed the soldier past the front desk, through a door and a short hallway, then into a small inner room. At the last minute he remembered to snatch off his blue-and-white cap.

"Colonel Maire? This is the boy asking for you."

An officer with iron-gray hair and colonel's insignia pushed a plate away from him on his desk and looked up. "Well?"

Jamal hesitated and glanced at the soldier who had brought him in.

The colonel sighed. "Leave us, Laval."

"Hmph," grunted the soldier and pulled the door shut behind him.

The colonel's eyes narrowed. "You have information about the spy? You'd better not be playing games with me, young man."

Jamal swallowed. He couldn't back down now. "That's just it, sir—David Hoffman *isn't* a spy *or* a traitor. I can prove it!"

"How?" The word popped more like a challenge than a question.

"Because, sir, I accidentally stumbled across him right here in Sefrou the same day the Legion marched for Taza."

The colonel's face remained hard, passive. "What time?"

"Uh, between noon and mid-afternoon prayers. I know because I had just come from school. He was hiding in an old vacant shop in the basket *suq*."

"So. You admit he deserted his regiment." Colonel Maire's eyes snapped fire. "A deserter *is* a traitor, young man! What is your name?"

"Um, Jamal, sir." He would leave his family name out of this as long as possible. "But a deserter who just doesn't want to fight is different than a spy who betrays his fellow soldiers and helps the other side—isn't that true? David Hoffman couldn't be your spy, because—"

"Why not?" Colonel Maire got to his feet, leaned over his desk, and pointed a finger at Jamal. "If Private Hoffman left right after roll call the night before, if he had a swift horse, he could have gotten to Abd el-Krim by dawn, spilled our plans, and gotten back here by the afternoon—when you found him."

Jamal was taken aback. What craziness was this? Why would a deserter come *back* to Sefrou once he'd gotten away? It made no sense! Besides . . . Jamal *knew* David had not left after roll call the night before, because David had still been in his bed after midnight. Jamal should know—he was there, creeping beside David's bed to steal his book!

But Jamal felt like a desert cat, caught with a boulder at its back and hunting dogs yapping in its face. If he admitted he had snuck into the soldiers' quarters that night, he would surely be arrested for trespassing and thieving!

"I don't know why you are trying to protect this prisoner—but I don't have time for this nonsense. Hoffman was the only soldier who deserted that day and *someone* warned el-Krim that reinforcements were coming, and from where." The colonel strode to the door and opened it. "Corporal Laval?" he yelled. "Show this boy out."

The soldier from the front desk sneered at Jamal as he took the boy's arm and hurried him from the office and out the front door. As the door slammed shut behind him, he sank miserably onto the ground beside the door, his head in his hands. What was he going to do? If the colonel didn't believe him, David was going to die!

Something he'd tucked in his cloth sash dug in his side as Jamal sat hopelessly outside the Legion office. He dug out the packet of Jesus pictures David had given him through the cell window earlier that afternoon. He almost felt like flinging the whole lot to the ground. Who cared about the stupid game now?

But instead he held them up to the fading light and squinted at the one on top. It was the picture of Jesus hanging on the cross with nails in His hands and feet. What was it David claimed Jesus had said to him in his dream? "I did it for you."

Suddenly Jamal's mind began to clear. Miss Cary said Jesus came from heaven to sacrifice His life, to pay the penalty for our sin, so he—Jamal Isaam—could live eternally with God.

Jamal straightened and stood up. If Jesus was willing to do that for him . . . if David was willing to get caught so Jamal wouldn't get in trouble for having the pictures . . .

With a surge of determination, Jamal marched back through the front door, right past the surprised corporal who had his feet up on the desk, down the hall, and to the colonel's office. The door was open, so Jamal let himself in. Before the colonel could say anything, Jamal blurted, "I know David Hoffman did not leave Sefrou that night because I saw him with my own eyes in his bed just past midnight." There. He'd said it. Now the colonel would have to admit that even with the swiftest horse, there was no way a foreign legion soldier could have ridden to Taza and back by noon the next day.

A firm hand quickly grabbed the back of Jamal's shirt. "I'm sorry, sir! The boy barged right in before I could stop him."

To Jamal's surprise, the colonel waved the man out of the room. But he wasn't surprised by the colonel's next question. "And *pourquoi,* may I ask, were *you* in the soldiers' sleeping quarters in the middle of the night? What mischief were you up to?"

Jamal steeled himself. There was no way to avoid trouble now. Almost unconsciously he sent a prayer heavenward: *Jesus, help me!* He startled himself. Why did he pray that? All he knew was that Jesus would understand.

As briefly as he could, Jamal admitted sneaking into the sleeping quarters to steal David Hoffman's book to get points for the game he'd invented.

"Likely story! Did anyone see you who could prove you were there?" the colonel demanded.

Jamal shook his head, thinking about the sleeping soldier. "But," he said, a little proudly, "I did steal his book. Just ask David Hoffman."

"No one saw you? Then you could be making this all up. As for David Hoffman—sure, he's going to agree with your story if it lets him off the hook. Now go away. I'm busy."

Jamal was shocked. The colonel still didn't believe him! His mind scrambled. He *had* been seen . . . by his uncle. But then the colonel would want to know what his uncle was doing hanging around the French garrison at midnight! Jamal was willing to risk his own neck, but he couldn't tell on his uncle. Besides, he didn't really know his uncle's business with the bearded sergeant—

"Wait! There *is* someone who saw me. One of your soldiers—a sergeant. He had light-colored hair and beard. Maybe he was on guard duty that night. He grabbed me as I was running past this office, but I got away. Ask him! He will tell you I was here. He'll know what time it was."

The colonel frowned. "Could be a dozen such men in this unit. Anything unusual about him?"

Jamal shrugs. "Not really. He swore at me in German. But he must be very good at languages. I heard him talking to someone else in one of the Berber dialects."

The colonel's eyes glinted. "You say he spoke *Berber*? But he swore at you in German?" The colonel opened the drawer of his desk and pulled out a picture. "Is this the man who saw you?"

It was the sergeant Jamal had seen that night. "Yes, yes! That's the man."

The colonel's face darkened in anger, and he spit out just one word: "Klem!"

Jamal was bewildered. Klem? Why was that name familiar? And then he remembered: *Sergeant Joseph Klem,* the infamous deserter who had joined ranks with Abd el-Krim, the Desert Prince, and aided his successful march against French outposts all that past month. So! It was Sergeant *Klem* who had come into Sefrou to spy out the Legion's plans and sped back to Taza to tell el-Krim. What role his uncle played, Jamal didn't know. They had been talking together, but at least he didn't have to tell on his uncle to save David Hoffman.

"The nerve of that traitor!" Colonel Maire snarled, banging a fist on his desk. "Using his uniform—the uniform he has desecrated—to walk right in here unnoticed!" He seemed to have forgotten Jamal. Striding into the small hallway, he roared: "Corporal Laval!" The soldier at the front desk scurried to the colonel's side. "Get me the officers who served on the military tribunal. Now!"

"But . . . but, sir, they're off duty. I don't—"

"Fool! We have a firing squad at dawn tomorrow morning that needs to be stopped. You have one hour!"

Weak with relief, Jamal put on his cap and started out the door, confident that justice would be done. But the colonel nailed him with a piercing glance. "Where do you think you're going? I need your testimony. Sit."

Jamal sat. He knew his family would be worried about him by now. He'd missed both evening prayer and the evening meal. What in the world was he going to tell them?

And then he realized it was simple: He would just tell them the truth . . . about The Game . . . about sneaking out of the house and stealing David's book . . . about hiding David in his room . . .

He'd just leave Uncle Samir out of it. Uncle Samir would have to be responsible for himself. It was going to be hard enough owning up to all the things *he* was responsible for.

Three officers showed up, irritability mixed with curiosity evident in their faces. David Hoffman was brought from the stockade, his hands and ankles in chains, and the hearing began.

Once again Jamal had to tell his story. A small smile played on David's face as he listened. The officers pelted Jamal with questions, much like the colonel had, but his answers were the same. And, like Colonel Maire, the officers were furious when they realized that Sergeant Joseph Klem—the Legion's "Most Wanted" deserter—had been prowling the garrison the night in question.

The tribunal conferred; it didn't take them long to reach a verdict. "Private David Hoffman, the charge against you for spying and delivering classified information to the enemy has been changed to simple desertion, and your sentence of death by firing squad has been commuted to two years of prison and hard labor." *Crack!* went the gavel.

Two years of prison and hard labor! Jamal's elation turned to dismay. But before he had time to catch David's eye to see how David felt about it, one of the officers said, "One moment. Colonel Maire, what about bringing charges against the boy? By his own admission, he is guilty of trespassing and stealing."

Jamal felt the hair on the back of his neck stand up. He'd known he was taking a risk by telling the truth, but—

"As far as I'm concerned," Colonel Maire growled, "the boy has kept us from committing a grave injustice. I'm not interested in pressing charges for trespassing. As far as the charge of stealing—that's up to Private Hoffman. Hoffman?"

A huge grin stretched ear to ear on David Hoffman's angular face. "No, sir! But I would like to talk to Jamal a moment before I go back to the stockade."

With a curt nod, the colonel and the other officers left, leaving only a guard with David and Jamal.

David's eyes were moist, but his smile was non-stop. "*Merci,* Jamal. You have literally saved my life! But, *pourquoi*? You took a great risk."

Jamal grinned, too. "You already know the answer!" He pulled out his packet of forbidden pictures and pointed to the picture on top—Jesus on the cross. "Because he did it for me."

Chapter 13

Epilogue

"Miss Cary is back!" "Miss Cary is back!" The word spread like wildfire among the children of Sefrou as a middle-aged woman wearing a "foreign" dress that hung several inches above her socks and sensible shoes—modest by American standards in 1928—climbed out of the battered truck cab and resettled her hat. With one hand holding on to her hat and the other shielding her eyes from the brilliant April sun, the woman tipped her head back and took a big breath, as if drinking in the musty smell of the camels and goats tethered outside the city gate. "Oh, Jamal! It's so good to be back home!"

A tall young man of fifteen

swung down off the back of the truck, grinning. "Me too, Miss Cary! Two years of school in the big city is enough for me!" Jamal Isaam, taller now but still sporting a boyish grin, began helping the truck driver unload bundles and boxes from the back of the truck. But even before he had time to locate a pushcart, Muslim and Jewish children were swarming out of the gate and around the American missionary.

"Are you going to teach classes again, Miss Cary?"

"Will you tell us some more Jesus stories?"

Some of the older boys saw commercial opportunity. "I'll help pull that cart, Miss Cary—only a small coin."

Somehow all the bundles and bags got loaded precariously onto a single cart, and the strange procession began winding its way through the familiar crowded streets. Jamal's happiness at being back home was tinged with some anxiety. So much had happened in the last three years!

Jamal's parents and grandfather had been astonished and dismayed to hear about The Game and all its consequences. The Jesus pictures had been destroyed and all the items belonging to the Legion returned—though recalling the puzzled expression on the colonel's face when he was handed a button belonging to *"le prisonnier"* gave the Isaam family many good laughs.

It didn't take long for the Desert Prince and his tribal warriors to push almost to the gates of Fez— but they had hesitated, fearing a trap. Those months had given the French time to regroup, and the following spring Abd el-Krim was driven back as quickly as he had advanced and was forced to sign a document of surrender. El-Krim was exiled and the rebellion had crumbled. Morocco as a "Protectorate" was once again firmly in the hands of the French, and Mohammed V had been appointed as the new sultan.

Once the siege of the royal city had lifted, Jamal had been sent to school in Fez to study Islamic law in hopes that he would quit all the nonsense that had been put in his head. Jamal had studied hard—he knew his family hoped he would follow in the steps of Grandfather Hatim—but he often thought about Miss Cary and the stories she'd told, and the Jewish soldier and his Hebrew New Testament. These two people were hardly the infidels—the enemies—he'd been led to believe foreigners to be.

While Jamal was at school, he was glad to read in the Moroccan newspaper that Sultan Mohammed V supported the nationalist movement for a free Morocco. *That* would give something for the French to worry about. But deep in Jamal's spirit, even though he didn't yet have the words to express it, a free Morocco also meant a free heart to seek the truth about God.

To his surprise, the two American missionaries he'd seen debating in the marketplace in Sefrou— Mr. Enyart and Mr. Swanson—showed up in the marketplaces of Fez! He stopped to listen and was invited to come to the Gospel Missionary Union house in Fez to study the Bible in Arabic. It was here he heard that Miss Cary, after burying her ailing parents in Kansas, was returning to Morocco. He had asked—and been granted—the privilege of accompanying her from Fez back to Sefrou.

As the procession ended up at the door of Miss Cary's house—as everyone called the modest house that had waited for her return—Maude Cary handed out coins to her helpers and candy to the little ones and shooed them away. "Come back tomorrow!" she laughed. "Right now I need to get off my feet."

The children scurried away as Jamal helped the missionary unload the cart. He noticed that her limp was worse than usual and insisted she sit down while he finished bringing in the boxes and bundles.

When he brought in the last of the bundles, she had a fire going in the brazier and a pot of water heating for tea. She sat on a box, hands on her knees, and gave Jamal a tired smile. "Oh, Jamal, see how hungry the children are? Back home our churches are full of young men and women with strong backs who call themselves Christians. Isn't it a shame that I have had to come back here alone? Oh, how we need workers—especially young men! There's so much I can't do—"

She was interrupted by a loud knock on the front door. "I'll get it, Miss Cary," said Jamal. "You just rest."

Jamal opened the front door, expecting to see more curious children—but his mouth fell open in delight. There stood Hameem, stocky as ever, solid as a man; behind him stood a soldier in a French

Foreign Legion uniform. "Hameem!" he shouted, slapping his old friend on both arms. "Ha ha! How did you know I was home?"

Before Hameem could answer, the soldier stepped forward and held out his hand in greeting. "*Bonjour,* Jamal. Remember me?"

Jamal's eyes widened. "David Hoffman." He swallowed, trying to find his voice. "You are no longer *le prisonnier.* But what are you doing here?"

"I heard that a Christian missionary had returned to Sefrou; Hameem offered to show me where she lives. You see, Jamal, I believe in Jesus from reading this book"—he held up the well-worn Hebrew New

Testament—"but I want to learn more about Him."

From the small courtyard within, Jamal heard the plaintive voice of Miss Cary. "Are you going to keep my guests all to yourself, Jamal?"

Laughing and talking, Jamal ushered the two visitors into Miss Cary's courtyard. Miss Cary insisted they sit down—"Will the floor do? I haven't any chairs or cushions yet!"—and offered them sweet mint tea in cups she'd dug out of a box. Hameem squirmed and shook his head—then his eyes widened as he saw Jamal lift the teacup to his lips.

"Jamal! What are you doing? It's the fast of Ramadan!"

Jamal looked at Miss Cary for support, drew a deep breath, and said quietly, "I no longer keep the fast of Ramadan. I have become a Christian."

Hameem's mouth fell open. Then he hunched his shoulders and stared at the floor for a long moment. He looked up. "Does your family know this?"

Jamal shook his head. "Not yet. But today . . . today I will tell them."

Hameem looked genuinely frightened. "Jamal! Do you know what this will mean? You could be disowned by your own family! No one will give you a job!"

Jamal nodded soberly. Oh yes, he had thought about this many times. "But, Hameem, I cannot be a secret Christian. Because Jesus is the Truth."

David Hoffman, sitting cross-legged on the floor, had been intently listening to this exchange. He set down his cup and sighed. "I am ashamed. You see,

Miss Cary, my grandfather is a very devout Jew, but my father no longer believes anything. I have never written to my family back in Poland about my belief in the Messiah because I am afraid they will disown me—will never let me come home." He looked with new respect at the younger boy. "But if Jamal has the courage to tell his family and face the persecution he is sure to suffer right here, I must find the courage to do the same."

Hameen hung his head. "I have wanted to believe, too—ever since I heard the stories Miss Cary told," he said in a small voice. "But I was afraid."

A well of happiness started deep in Jamal's spirit and grew until he felt like shouting. Instead, he reached into the folds of his *jellaba* and pulled out a picture of Jesus on the cross, a new one given to him by the missionaries in Fez.

"Here, Hameem, keep this. Think about why Jesus died. Because . . . He did it for you."

More About Maude Cary

In 1901, twenty-three-year-old Maude Cary sailed for Morocco with four other young Americans—all single—to help bring the Gospel to the Muslim people. The Gospel Missionary Union worked in co-operation with four other Protestant missions in Morocco to put the unwritten language of the no-madic Berber tribes into writing, to translate por-tions of Scripture into Arabic, and to reach Muslim men with the Gospel in the marketplace and the women in the home. Summer months were spent doing evangelism among the many villages.

Maude's early years as a missionary were diffi-cult. She outscored one of her male peers in language study, and her "gaiety, friendliness, and laughter" and "pride of dress" brought criticism down on her head that she was worldly, lacked meekness, and was too flighty. The mission board suggested she go home—but she clung to her calling, refusing to go unless they actually sent her away. Soon she was assigned to the mission in El Ksar. Other missions were opened up in Meknes and Sefrou.

Many years passed, filled with language study, translation of the Scriptures, and sharing the Gospel to a polite but indifferent people, with no conversions among the Muslim people—only several Jewish boys. Outwardly polite, Moroccans despised the missionaries on two levels: because they preached the Christian Gospel, and because of the foreign nations they represented. Colonialism was at its fever pitch in Africa at the turn of the century, and the French had been pushing for a toehold in Morocco for years to help keep its hold on neighboring Algiers. Although the sultan was the official ruler of Morocco, he held only a nominal control of the fertile coastal area west of the Atlas Mountains. Elsewhere, especially among the fiercely independent Berber tribes to the east, the sultan's rule was largely ignored.

In 1907, French forces occupied Morocco, launching their offensive from Casablanca, and in 1912, Sultan Hafid signed the Treaty of Fez, making Morocco a French protectorate.

Meanwhile, several single men and women of the Gospel Missionary Union became married couples, and this was Maude's dream—to not only be a missionary but a wife and mother, as well. George Reed, secretary of the mission, asked her to be his wife— but the prolonged engagement was broken in 1913 when George left Morocco to establish a GMU mission in the Sudan. Maude's heart was broken, but at least now she knew where she stood. She had nothing to hold her back from giving one hundred percent to mission work.

As the men of the mission pushed into new frontiers, Maude was often left to take care of things by herself in Meknes and Sefrou—teaching classes to boys, teaching Arabic to new (often young) missionaries, and assisting at births and bedsides of sick missionaries, even though her own health often failed. She divided much of her time between the two locations: in Meknes, the sultan donated a house to the missionaries, which they called "Three Derb Skat"; in Sefrou, the mission house was known simply as "Miss Terri's house" ("Terri" possibly being a mispronunciation of "Cary").

In 1914, war broke out in Europe and many French battalions were recalled to France. Those soldiers who were left in Morocco were bitter and restless. They were prevented from fighting in "The Great War" and also forbidden to do anything in Morocco except "hold" the territory already occupied. The French Resident General, Marshal Louis Lyautey, threw himself into public works: building roads and harbors, establishing schools and infirmaries, even setting up a merry-go-round in Fez! "Much was done *for* the Moroccans, but little done *by* them," wrote one biographer.

After the war, the French and the unruly Berber tribes engaged in "bush warfare." The French would advance in the spring and summer, build a blockhouse in the new area in the fall, then leave a few Legionnaires to hold the fort till spring. These forts were regularly ambushed by rebel forces among the Berbers. French morale was at an all-time low.

As for the missionaries, by 1924 there were five baptized believers among the tribespeople—the fruit of a quarter of a century of work! Persecution from tribe and family was relentless, but the believers held firm. In Sefrou, Maude had reason to be encouraged. She had the respect of the local women—they appreciated the simple medicines with which she doctored them, and she did all she could to alleviate hunger and poverty. Dozens of Jews also came to hear the Word preached and debate matters of religion.

In April of 1925, a serious rebellion developed among the tribespeople under the leadership of Abd el-Krim—aided by a French deserter, Sgt. Joseph Klem, as advisor. El-Krim steamrollered his way south across the country, capturing nine French border outposts, while another thirty were evacuated. French forces rushed to hold Taza, a small town not far from Sefrou. El-Krim turned his forces and pushed all the way to Fez, one of the royal cities, but hesitated, fearing a trap. This gave the French time to regroup.

Maude had been in Morocco twenty-three years without a break (the missionaries had come for life), but she finally took a furlough to assist her aging parents. She stayed with her elderly parents for three years, but when they died, she returned in 1928 to her beloved Sefrou in Morocco. To her joy, two young men—formerly boys in her classes—took their stand as Christians: Mehdi Ksara and Mohammed Bouabid, even though it meant fierce opposition from their families.

Around this time another young man appeared at the mission door: Leon Hoffman, another French deserter. He had been caught, but while in prison, he read a Hebrew New Testament and one night saw a vision of Christ holding out his nail-scarred hands, saying: "I died for *your* sins." Leon was so moved that he determined to find some Christians to help him understand what it all meant. Realizing the spiritual hunger of the young Legionnaires in Morocco, the GMU missionaries set up special meetings to reach out to them with the Gospel.

Like Mehdi and Mohammed, Leon was also disowned by his relatives back in Poland. All three young men became faithful workers with Maude Cary and the Gospel Missionary Union. (Leon came back to Morocco after his tour of duty with the French Foreign Legion was completed.)

Maude Cary took a second furlough in 1936 and returned a year later. Health problems and family needs had taken a toll on many of the GMU missionaries. As the world prepared for another war, two more single women missionaries slipped into the country before the door slammed shut—leaving only Maude and three other women to maintain three mission houses (Meknes, Sefrou, and Khemisset) and carry on the work. Rather than huddle together for support, they spread out—and when the war was over, the work was still alive, thanks to these courageous women!

After World War II, Maude prayed "for at least ten men" to work among Muslim men. But even after her prayer was answered, Maude didn't slow down. At the age of seventy-one, she opened a new mission at El Hajeb, in spite of poor health and much opposition. "The work is prospering," she quipped, "as one can tell by the battered front door."

The undercurrents for Moroccan independence exploded again in 1953. The French sent Sultan Mohammed V (Sidi Mohammed Ben Yousef) into exile, but it only fanned the flames of rebellion. In 1955, Mohammed V was brought back from exile—just as Maude Cary, who was very ill, took her final trip back home to the United States. The next year the sultan negotiated independence from France and gave himself the title of "King."

In 1967, Maude Cary died at the age of eighty-eight in Kansas—just as all missionaries were ordered to leave Morocco. They were given eight days to pack and get out. Mission houses had to be abandoned. After seventy-five years of service, there were no GMU missionaries (or any Christian missionaries) in Morocco. Now the Gospel was in the hands of the Moroccan Christians like Mehdi Ksara and Mohammed Bouabid.

For Further Reading

Stenbock, Evelyn. *"Miss Terri!": The Story of Maude Cary, Pioneer GMU Missionary in Morocco.* (England: Back to the Bible Broadcast, 1970).

For more exciting stories from Dave and Neta Jackson, read any of their four *Hero Tales* collections. Here's an excerpt from *Volume IV*:

TOM WHITE

A Really "Bad" Bible Boy

Tom White didn't plan to go to prison, but he couldn't let go of what he'd learned about Christians suffering for their faith. In the 1970s officials from Communist countries were telling the world that they allowed religious freedom. But Tom kept learning that many Christians in those countries were beaten, imprisoned, or even killed for preaching the Gospel.

Russian and Cuban pastors coming to the Free World on *official* tours sometimes claimed to enjoy complete freedom. But they never brought their families, and they evaded direct questions about Christians imprisoned for their faith or Bibles that had been confiscated or churches that had been closed or destroyed by the government.

The more Communist officials—and even some church officials in the United States—claimed that there was religious freedom in these countries, the more the reports of oppression and persecution increased. Tom met with Cuban refugees, and the stories were consistent—even from unbelievers: The government did everything possible to stamp out Christianity.

Why didn't more Americans know this? "Westerners truly want to believe the best of people," Tom White concluded. "While this is an admirable trait, when carried to the extreme, it becomes willful ignorance."

So Tom committed himself to two tasks: supporting persecuted Christians around the world and letting the Free World know about their suffering.

Cuba was not far away, and Christians there needed gospel literature, so Tom joined with other Christians to provide it. To get the Gospel to the people in a country where distributing Christian literature was prohibited, they packaged it in waterproof plastic baggies and dropped thousands of them into the sea off the coast of Cuba so that the ocean currents would carry them ashore. Later, Tom made flights over Cuba, dropping similar packets from a plane, distributing over four hundred thousand pieces of Christian literature.

But on May 27, 1979, his small plane crash-landed in Cuba after he finished a night drop. He and his pilot were arrested, interrogated (under torture), and sentenced to twenty-four years in prison.

After three months in solitary confinement, Tom was moved into the main prison population of seven thousand, where he met and worshiped with many members of the Cuban church who were imprisoned for their faith.

Extensive prayer and international appeals from U.S. Congressmen, Mother Teresa, and others finally secured Tom and his pilot's release after only seventeen months in prison.

Upon returning to the United States, Tom White became the director of The Voice of the Martyrs, an organization that encourages and supports persecuted Christians around the world. The Voice of the Martyrs has identified over forty countries where persecution of Christians is overlooked or even encouraged by the government. While not officially condoned, persecution of Christians occurs in many other locations around the world, as well. According to a Regent University study, some 156,000 Christians were martyred in 1995, more than in the entire first century.

FAITH
"Mayday! Mayday! We're Going Down!"

~~~~~~~~~~~~~~~~~~~~~~~~~~~~~~~~

The small plane bucked and stumbled through the rough night air as it strained toward the lightning-laced thunderheads. "We've got to go around," yelled the pilot, Mel Bailey, over the roar of the engine.

"But look at our gas." Tom White's hand floated up and down and side to side as he tried to point to the gas gauges. "We'll never make it!"

Having just crossed over Cuba, they were heading toward Jamaica. But their time over Cuba had been far more than the most direct path from Florida to Jamaica. While Mel guided the plane through the night sky on May 27, 1979, Tom had dumped seventeen boxes of Christian literature out the door. Thousands and thousands of tracts fluttered to the ground to be picked up by people who had never heard about Jesus in this country where the Communist government opposed the Gospel.

But the plane no sooner turned away from the face of the thunderclouds than its navigational equipment stopped working. Tom and Mel flew on through the dark night until, rising out of a sea shimmering in the lightning, they could make out what looked like the dark mass of an island. Mel began calling on the radio to the airport in Montego Bay for instructions. The airport controllers said they were flashing their runway lights, but the only lights Tom and Mel saw on the ground remained steady and looked like the lights of villages, not a runway.

Suddenly the engine sputtered and died—out of gas.

"Montego," said Mel into his microphone, "we're heading toward some lights, coming straight in."

"Roger," said the controller. "We'll send out the fire trucks, but we still haven't spotted you visually or on radar."

As Mel and Tom continued to descend, there were fewer and fewer options. "There," Tom said, pointing through the dark. "I think that's a highway. Let's land on it."

Mel banked the plane and squinted at the road illumined by the lights from occasional houses and streetlights. "There? But there's people along it."

"They'll get out of the way when they see we are in trouble and coming in."

Again, Mel grabbed the mike. "Mayday. Mayday. Mayday. We're going in on a country road, but I don't know where! Mayday!"

Mel then concentrated on guiding the plane to a perfect landing on the narrow road.

With the wheels still about a foot off the ground, Tom raised his hand in warning, but it was too late. The right wing smashed into a dump truck that was parked to the side. The plane spun around, then twisted and tumbled down the road for four hundred yards until it screeched to a stop upside down.

Amazingly, neither Tom nor Mel was injured or even bruised, but when they climbed out of the plane, they discovered that the people who came running up all spoke Spanish.

They were in Cuba, not Jamaica!

Within moments the G–2 police came racing through the crowd and arrested Tom and Mel. Would they be thrown in prison or tortured or shot? Who would know where they were? How could anyone help them?

"Well," said Tom to Mel as they waited to see what would

happen to them, "the King of the universe was riding with us when we crashed. He'll continue to be with us even in Cuba. Just hang on to Him and take each moment as it comes."

Faith is hanging on to Jesus when all else seems lost.

FROM GOD'S WORD:
Let us look only to Jesus, the One who began our faith and who makes it perfect (Hebrews 12:2a).

LET'S TALK ABOUT IT:
1. Why do you think Tom White thought it was so important to get the Gospel to people in Cuba?
2. Why did Tom and Mel have faith that God would take care of them after they were arrested?
3. Can you think of any people who took a great risk or paid a high price to make the Bible available to us? Tell how.